FISH IN A DOUBLE-BARREL

"I've got another itch for that woman that I'm going to take care of right now."

Longarm stepped in front of Victoria and his words were deadly. "I don't think so."

The man's jaw dropped in amazement, and he was ridiculously slow in making a stab for his gun. Longarm pulled one of the triggers of the shotgun and it exploded like a Civil War cannon. The outlaw with the "itch" was lifted completely off the ground and nearly torn apart by the blast. Longarm shifted the barrels and fired again and two more outlaws were knocked down like wheat in a high wind.

Includes an excerpt from

BUSHWHACKERS

The all-new, all-action Western series
from the creators of
Longarm

Available in paperback from Jove Books

DON'T MISS THESE
ALL-ACTION WESTERN SERIES
FROM THE BERKLEY PUBLISHING GROUP

THE GUNSMITH by J. R. Roberts
Clint Adams was a legend among lawmen, outlaws, and ladies. They called him . . . the Gunsmith.

LONGARM by Tabor Evans
The popular long-running series about U.S. Deputy Marshal Long—his life, his loves, his fight for justice.

SLOCUM by Jake Logan
Today's longest-running action Western. John Slocum rides a deadly trail of hot blood and cold steel.

BUSHWHACKERS by B. J. Lanagan
An all-new series by the creators of Longarm! The rousing adventures of the most brutal gang of cutthroats ever assembled—Quantrill's Raiders.

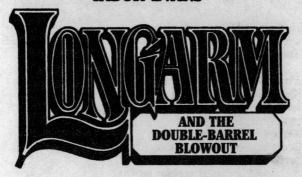

TABOR EVANS

LONGARM

AND THE DOUBLE-BARREL BLOWOUT

JOVE BOOKS, NEW YORK

LONGARM AND THE DOUBLE-BARREL BLOWOUT

A Jove Book / published by arrangement with
the author

PRINTING HISTORY
Jove edition / July 1997

The Putnam Berkley World Wide Web site address is
http://www.berkley.com

ISBN: 0-515-12104-5

A JOVE BOOK®
Jove Books are published by The Berkley Publishing Group,
200 Madison Avenue, New York, New York 10016.
JOVE and the "J" design are trademarks
belonging to Jove Publications, Inc.

PRINTED IN THE UNITED STATES OF AMERICA

10 9 8 7 6 5 4 3 2 1

Chapter 1

When the small and very rumpled package landed on his littered desk, United States Deputy Marshal Custis Long paid it no attention as he struggled to complete some detested federal paperwork. By four o'clock, however, Custis had finally cleared his desk enough to rediscover the messy brown package. It caught his attention among a number of other unopened packages precisely because it was battered and disreputable looking.

When Longarm held it up for a closer inspection, he began searching for a postmark but it had been partially smudged. As best he could tell, the brown, string-tied package had been mailed from somewhere in Arizona. Whoever had addressed it was damn lucky because the package was inadequately addressed to LONGARM, U.S. GOVNMINT, DENVIR, COLORADOE.

No department. No street address.

"Watch out for that one," a passing federal worker

remarked. "Looks like it could hold a rattlesnake or some Indian curse."

Longarm shook his head and massaged the package. "Nope. Nothing moving. Nothing to worry about."

The man chuckled. "Then it might be some poison from one of your frontier women who discovered that you have a girlfriend in every town between St. Louis and San Francisco."

"Oh, bullshit."

It was obvious that Marshal Slim Behan was at loose ends with nothing of his own to do. The man was bored and loitering beside Custis's desk waiting for him to open the package.

"Haven't you got something of your own to do?" Longarm finally asked.

Slim sauntered over to his own desk, yelling back over his shoulder, "Hope it's bad news, Longarm. You been having too damn much fun the last couple of times you went out."

"Sure I have! If your idea of 'fun' is getting shot in the shorts and almost beaten to death by a couple of murdering whores I had to deliver to the federal prison."

"Ha! I seen them whores! Was four of 'em and they were all kissing you good-bye and trying to unbuckle your belt one last time! Some hardship assignment, you lucky bastard."

"They weren't trying to get into my pants! They were trying to get into my *pockets* so they could remove their handcuffs!"

"Sure they were!"

The entire office began to laugh, and Custis could feel his cheeks warming so he decided to call it a day. Snatching up the little envelope and his snuff-brown and

2

flat-crowned Stetson, Longarm barreled for the door, and his exit caused even more laughter.

Longarm felt better the minute he was outside. The spring weather was invigorating and the trees in the nearby park were bursting with pale green leaves and sweet-smelling blossoms. The air was like perfume and so clear that to Longarm even the most distant snow-capped peaks seemed magnified and almost touchable. The day was a tonic and, best of all, Longarm was about to go on vacation.

Vacation. Even the word sounded strange because he hadn't had one in so many years. Oh, sure, his friend and supervisor, Billy Vail, certainly *wanted* to give Custis a well deserved rest. It had been two years since Custis had taken any time off and he was mentally exhausted and physically exhausted. But their office was chronically shorthanded and Longarm, being the best and most experienced field marshal, was impossible to replace on the toughest cases. But *this* June, by damned, he was going on vacation. Maybe to New Orleans or St. Louis or even back to West Virginia where he still had a few relatives.

"Hey, Custis!" Ruben, the shoe shine man, called. "Need your boots worked on today?"

Ruben had been shining Longarm's boots for years. The old man claimed to be part Apache Indian, and probably was, for his skin was the color of leather. Ruben was a colorful character and liked to wear a red bandanna like Cochise or Geronimo. His hair was straight and black, streaked liberally with silver hair and always bound in a pair of thick braids. Ruben had a great fondness for turquoise and silver jewelry. He liked to talk while he worked and his favorite customers were the frontier marshals that moved in and out of Denver's federal building.

"My boots look pretty good, Ruben."

"I can make 'em look even better."

"All right," Longarm said, knowing that Ruben would be hurt if Longarm failed to tell him that he was about to go on a monthlong vacation.

"Longarm, you jest sit right down and take a load off these feet. Wanna read yesterday's newspaper?"

"No thanks," Longarm said, stepping up onto the chair and resting his boots on iron pegs. "I'm going on vacation next week. Thought I'd let you know so you didn't think someone out there plugged me this time."

"A vacation!" Ruben grinned, always an interesting sight because of his missing front teeth. "Where you goin'?"

"Haven't decided for sure," Longarm admitted. "Maybe New Orleans. Think I'd like to take the train to St. Louis and then ride the riverboats all the way down to the Gulf of Mexico."

"Woo-wee! Now maybe you need old Ruben to come along and carry your bags and to keep these boots lookin' good!"

"I couldn't afford you," Longarm said as he gave Ruben the customary five-cent cheroot and stuck one in his own mouth. He lit both and the two men puffed in contentment for a moment before Ruben started dabbing on brown shoe polish, saying, "That sure is a sorry-lookin' little package you got there, Longarm. What's in it?"

"Damned if I know. I guess I might as well find out."

Ruben nodded to indicate he also thought that was probably a good idea. "Where's it from?"

"Arizona, if I'm reading this smudged postmark correctly."

Longarm reached for his pocketknife. He was a big man, standing six four and weighing over two hundred pounds. He was still in his prime and cut an imposing figure with his deeply tanned face, broad shoulders, and handlebar mustache. He had a notorious reputation as a ladies' man, and not without good reason, although he never spoke of his times with women nor did he give them much thought when he was hot on some outlaw's trail.

Longarm cut the package string. "Ruben, this package is so beat-up it looks as if it's probably been stomped on by a bunch of your Apache."

"If it was from *my* Apache relatives, it'd be wrapped in a white man's scalp!"

Longarm chuckled and began to open the package. The outer brown paper peeled away to reveal a neatly folded newspaper.

"Yep," Longarm drawled. "It's from Arizona. *Wickenburg Weekly Press.* Exactly a month old to the day."

"Someone sent you a newspaper all the way from Arizona?"

Longarm spread the paper across his lap. He was surprised to find that there was nothing inside of it, but one of the articles was circled by a wavery pencil mark. Ruben forgot about the shoes and came around behind Longarm to stare at the paper.

"I *been* in Wickenburg. Hotter'n Flagstaff but not as bad as Tucson. There's a few Apache and Mojave people there, but none of 'em belong to my family."

"Well, I sure don't know anyone from Wickenburg."

"Maybe you should read that paper," Ruben suggested. "Maybe someone you know died there . . . or got rich!"

"Maybe," Longarm said. "I suppose that Wickenburg is a mining town."

"Rough as they come."

Longarm refolded the paper and smoked in silence. Ruben's hands and shine rag always made his tired feet feel better and that alone was enough of a reason to pay the man even when his boots weren't scuffed or muddy.

"I lived in Arizona for twenty-six years," Ruben said. "My family worked in a silver mine near Tucson, then raised some sheep and we caught wild horses to sell to the same damn army that put us on reservations."

"Some of you deserved it," Longarm said. "Although I'm sure that didn't include your family."

"Yeah, it did," Ruben admitted. "My family was bad. Real bad. Most of my uncles and my father were all either shot or hanged. I'd have been too, if I hadn't cleared out fast."

"But I thought you once told me you and a couple of brothers went all the way to Washington, D.C."

"We did. Went there to talk to the Great White Father. We were gonna tell him that the Apache deserved fair and honest treatment. We had been given a treaty, but it was broken by the white soldiers."

"And what did the President say?"

Ruben removed the cheroot and spat on the ground. "He wouldn't see us and so we got drunk. Raised hell and killed a couple of people fighting in a saloon. I got away, my brothers didn't. One of 'em, Charlie Big Thumbs, is still alive."

"And in prison after all these years?"

Ruben shook his head. "Charlie, he don't know nothin' no more. Some guard hit him once too often in

6

the head. I brought him to Denver to see a specialist. They put him in the big hospital. He eats good. Always laughing. I tried to take him out and he started howlin' like a coyote. Wouldn't leave!''

Longarm had never heard Ruben open up so completely. Up until this very minute, the man had always been a supreme enigma. ''And that's why you've stayed here in Denver?''

''That and the fact that I got a wife now and four kids. She's Ute, not Apache, but she can cook good and warms my bed. She won't go to Arizona and neither will my kids. If I go alone, maybe I get hanged. Arizona men are rough sons a bitches and don't care if their boots look good or not, so maybe I starve. Right?''

''That's right,'' Longarm said, still marveling that Ruben had opened up so completely.

Ruben's shine rag began to pop like a farm boy's rabbit rifle. ''You ain't going to ask me why I'd hang in Arizona, are you?''

''No.''

''Good! I killed a few men, but they deserved it. There's some real bastards livin' in Arizona; I put a few of the worst in their graves but never took a scalp.''

''Ruben, I've always wondered—how old are you?''

''Fifty . . . seven just last Tuesday.''

Longarm tried to hide his surprise. He'd thought that Ruben was at least seventy. The man's weathered face and bent body were the best evidence that he had lived a very hard and dangerous life.

''Someday,'' Ruben was saying, ''I'm gonna be shinin' your boots or someone else's, and the President will come by and see what a good job I do and want me to shine *his* shoes. And, when I do, I won't charge him nothin". That's right!''

Ruben's voice had taken on an angry tremor and now his rag really began to pop. "That's right, Marshal Long, I won't take a penny, but I will roast his ass over the broken treaties and them gawdamn reservations where all Indian people are treated worse'n stray dogs."

"Maybe he'll even make some changes," Longarm said, wanting to give Ruben hope.

"No, he won't. But I'll feel better for having given him a piece of my mind. And I'll tell my wife and kids and they'll tell all their friends and I'll be a big man . . . for a while."

"You sure will be," Longarm said, lapsing into a reverie.

"What does the Arizona paper say?"

"I don't know. Haven't read it yet."

"Can I have it after you're done? Maybe I'll read about someone I knew."

"Sure," Longarm said, deciding that he might as well read the article so he could just give the paper to Ruben. It would be one less thing that he'd have to try to remember tomorrow.

The circled article began by saying that an old prospector named Jim Cox had been found shot out in the desert but that he was recovering from his wounds.

"Jimmy is a good friend of mine," Longarm explained. "He saved my life a few years ago. Never forget him."

Ruben glanced up from Longarm's now glistening boots. "How'd he do that?"

"I was tracking a murdering outlaw down near Tucson. Nothing in his past warned me that he carried a big buffalo rifle and knew how to use it. From a half mile away, he ambushed and winged me in the leg; the same bullet passed through the belly of my horse. So there I was, about sixty miles from water with a leakin' leg and a dying horse.''

"But a man as experienced as you would have been carrying plenty of water.''

"Yeah, but that same damned slug went through my canteen. And I was pinned under the horse when it fell, and the outlaw decided it would be interesting to see if he could put another bullet through my horse into me. Follow?''

"I believe so.'' Ruben frowned. "So there you were, no water, dead horse lyin' on a leakin' leg, and this outlaw son of a bitch using you for target practice.''

"That's about the way it was,'' Longarm said. "I was in a terrible fix.''

"But then I suppose this Jim Cox showed up and killed the outlaw?''

"No,'' Longarm said, "but he ran him off and then he got me outta my scrape. I'd have died without Jimmy's help.''

"What ever happened to the outlaw?''

"Apache caught and tortured him to death about a week later over by Casa Grande. They tied him to a big cactus and burned him alive after they'd cut off a bunch of his body parts. He was a murdering son of a bitch, but even he didn't deserve that bad a death.''

"My people do know how to torture. But then, some whites are pretty good at it too.''

"Agreed.'' Longarm turned his attention back to the newspaper. "Maybe I better read on and find out the rest of Jim's story.''

Longarm read the remainder of the article out loud and it went on to say that Jim Cox, delirious with fever, had told a story of a lost Spanish treasure that he had been hunting for more than twenty years. No one had taken the story seriously. They'd considered it no more than the ranting of a fevered mind, until Cox had finally recovered, then paid all his bills with a handful of Spanish coins.

The golden coins created another kind of fever around Wickenburg. But by the time the news of them got around, Cox had vanished into the desert.

"Well, I'll be damned!" Longarm exclaimed. "I guess maybe old Jim *did* finally locate that lost Spanish treasure he'd been searching for over the last twenty years."

"He musta!" Excitement was high in Ruben's dark eyes. "Else, how else would he have had the coins?"

"I don't know. But what I can't understand is . . ."

Longarm's eye fell to a penciled note on the bottom of the page, so faintly written that he had almost overlooked it. Squinting, he read these words: AM ALMOST RICH BUT HUNTID LIKE AN ANAMAL. YOU *OWE* ME. HELP. COME SOON! JIMMY.

"Damn!" Longarm swore. "He's being hunted."

"Why, sure he is," Ruben said. "He's almost found a fortune in Spanish gold. Probably *has* found it by now. Probably been killed and robbed by now too."

Longarm reread the article, then folded it back up and stuffed it into his coat pocket. He lapsed into a troubled silence.

"What are you going to do now?" Ruben asked.

"I don't know."

"He saved your life, Custis, you got to at least try and return the favor."

"Yeah, but I'm going to New Orleans."

"No you're not," Ruben said. "Unless I've badly misjudged you, Marshal, you're headed for Wickenburg. New Orleans is still gonna be there for you someday."

10

Longarm swore under his breath. "Dammit, Ruben, I was just in Arizona last month!"

"Then you probably still got a couple of women waiting for you down there."

"Not very damn likely."

Ruben cackled. "Wish I could go along and see some of that Spanish treasure! Be a lot more fun than shinin' shoes and waiting for the President to show up someday."

"And about as likely," Longarm drawled. "Dammit, I don't want to go back to Arizona."

"You could get rich."

"Or dead."

"If this Jim Cox is still alive, you tell him to come live in Denver. We'll swap stories and have some good times on his money."

"I'll do that," Longarm promised, climbing to his feet and paying Ruben. "And, if Jimmy does come back, I'll make sure that he brings enough Spanish gold to keep us all going for the rest of our lives."

Ruben gave Longarm a big, toothless smile and then turned to a waiting customer, saying, "Best shine in Denver or the world. Just ten cents!"

"I sure admire the job you did on that big man's boots," a pudgy office worker said, taking Longarm's seat with a weary sigh. "If you do as good a job on mine, there's an extra nickel coming, Ruben."

Longarm dashed back into the federal building, hoping to catch Billy Vail and explain his change of plans for the coming weeks. Sure, he'd miss New Orleans and the big paddle wheel boats plying the Mississippi River, but the thought of a relaxing vacation had already vanished like smoke in a dry desert wind.

Chapter 2

United States Marshal Billy Vail kicked his feet up on his desk and tipped back his office chair as he stared at Longarm. When the big lawman had finished explaining why his plans to take a New Orleans vacation had suddenly been changed, Billy frowned.

"The thing of it is, Custis, you *need* a vacation. I was willing to let you go for a month because I knew that for years you've been taking the lion's share of the bad cases being assigned out of this office."

"I'm not complaining."

"Of course you're not. But the fact remains, this Wickenburg business isn't going to be a vacation. In fact, it sounds like another assignment. You know that Sonora Desert country is already heating up. It'll be hot and dangerous going down to Wickenburg and trying to save your friend's ass."

"I haven't any choice. I do owe the man my life."

"Yeah, yeah," Billy said, waving off the comment with his hand. "But you're also working on raw edges."

"I'm not anywhere at the end of my rope," Longarm said defensively. "And I can always take a few days off to rest after I get this Arizona business cleared up."

"You mean a sort of abbreviated vacation?"

"Sure. It just so happens that I have a good friend in Prescott, and it's pretty cool up there even in the summertime. New Orleans can wait until next year."

Billy frowned. "It's just that I *hate* the idea of you using up your vacation time trying to save this Jimmy Cox fella from being killed. It's plenty likely that it will require an entire month and then you'll have no time to relax in Prescott with that woman."

"I didn't *say* my friend was a woman."

"You didn't need to," Billy answered with a sly smile. "I saw something in your eyes that told me it was a she. Anyway, I have an idea."

Longarm got nervous whenever Billy had "an idea" because it almost always involved some federal business that no one else wanted to handle out of this office.

"Look," Longarm said, coming to his feet, "I appreciate your concern, but I do have a month of vacation coming and it starts tomorrow. So why don't you let me worry about how restful it's going to be?"

"My idea," Billy said, acting as if he hadn't been listening, "is that, if you were willing, I could give you a federal assignment in Arizona near where your friend was last seen. That way, you could combine your hunt with our business."

"Why should I do that?"

"Because you'd be a complete fool not to. And by that, I mean that if you agree to combine your business with that of the federal government, we'll forget that you are on vacation time and all your expenses will be covered."

Longarm's brow furrowed. There was, he knew, a catch in this somewhere. Billy was his friend, but he was always looking to cut his own operating budget and get the absolute most out of his field personnel.

"What do you say?" Billy asked.

"Naw," Longarm said, "I think I'll just do this on my own hook. That way, I won't have to worry about *two* problems."

"But what if you arrive in Wickenburg and quickly discover that the old prospector is dead? Or that he's just another old crackpot with too much time in the hot sun? Or that there is no Spanish treasure and that the whole thing is a hoax?"

"I'll take my chances," Longarm replied. "Jimmy Cox isn't the kind to play games. If he paid his bills with Spanish gold and said that he found treasure, then that's what he did."

"But the article says that he was delirious with a fever when he told that treasure story."

Longarm gave that a moment's thought before answering, "People *can't* lie when they are delirious. Jimmy has found his Spanish gold, all right. And there are plenty of people in Arizona that would kill their own mothers for a dollar just the same as there are anywhere else."

Billy ran his fingers through his thinning hair. The physical contrast between he and Longarm couldn't have been more striking. While Longarm was tall, broad-shouldered, and rugged, Billy looked soft, was twenty pounds overweight, and had the sweet, innocent face of an Irish priest. The fact was, however, that Billy was tough-minded and high-principled. He worked hard and was devoted to the capture and conviction of criminals who had sinned against mankind and the federal government.

"Tell you what," Billy offered. "This *job* that I have for you in Arizona won't take very long. No more than a couple of days. For that, *all* your travel expenses for the entire month will be covered. And . . . I'll kick in a little extra, if you'll bring our prisoner all the way back to Denver for trial."

"Who is he?"

"His name is Hank Bass."

"I've never heard of him."

"That's because he uses so many aliases. Bass is a hired gunman and sometimes bank robber. He works alone and has even been known to wear disguises."

"Where is his hangout?"

Vail removed his feet from his desk and leaned forward. "He seems to operate around Prescott. Isn't that where you said your lady friend lived?"

"I said that my *friend* lived there."

"Well, it's perfect then! Just arrest Hank Bass, have the local marshal hold him in jail, and then go about your own business helping this old prospector and getting reacquainted with your lady friend—all on government time . . . and money!"

When Longarm still hesitated, Billy pleaded, "Custis, you've everything to gain and nothing to lose! This is a sweet damn deal I'm offering. One that, if anyone else knew that you were already going to Arizona, could cause me no small amount of grief with my superiors."

"Tell me more about Hank Bass and then I'll decide whether or not to accept your generous offer."

"Not much to tell," Billy said with a shrug. "He's about your age, and, from what little we know, nothing much special. He's robbed several trains and taken government mail, so that's why we're so interested in getting him apprehended.''

"Why can't the local officials lock him up?''

Billy looked away for a moment. "Well,'' he said, trying to look unconcerned, "I guess Hank Bass has quite a reputation as a gunman. He's killed a number of marshals and even an Arizona Ranger. I hear that he's kinda quick with a Colt.''

Longarm's cheeks blew out and he came to his feet. "So there we have it,'' he said. "You're sending me after a gunslinger that has pretty well wiped out the opposition. He probably has a lot of friends who are also not being invited to the local church services because they are equally 'quick' with a Colt revolver. Am I getting the picture?''

"Yeah,'' Billy said, shoulders slumping. "Maybe I had just better go and get the job done myself.''

Vail looked so serious that Longarm almost believed him. And while he knew that Billy was a lot tougher than he appeared, Longarm also realized that the man had been in an office for the last five years and had probably lost his fighting edge, if not his fighting spirit.

"Or,'' Billy was saying, "I could send Slim Behan. He doesn't seem to have much to do right now.''

"Slim wouldn't stand a chance,'' Longarm replied. "And he *hates* the desert. He'd get down there and maybe ask a few questions. Then he'd dive into a saloon and spend all his expense money and have to wire you for more. In the end, you'd have to recall Slim and send me after I return from vacation.''

"Yeah,'' Billy agreed, "you're probably right. So why don't you accept my offer and save us all a lot of

16

time, money, and grief? I know that you could use the travel and expense money.''

"Sure I could, but . . ."

"I'll wire the marshal in Prescott and give him—" Billy stopped in mid-sentence, causing Longarm to blink and say, "What?"

"Oh, I just forgot that the marshal in Prescott was one of the ones that Hank Bass gunned down.''

"Aw, shit," Longarm growled. "What about Wickenburg?''

"I don't know," Billy said, looking doubtful. "It's got such a raw reputation that I doubt they've got a lawman there anymore either.''

Longarm expelled a deep breath. "All right," he said, pulling out his Ingersol pocket watch and consulting the time. "I've got a lot of packing and some details to follow up on this evening before I head out of town. How soon can you have the money?''

"Tomorrow afternoon?''

"Too late. You know as well as I do that the train leaves at noon.''

"Sorry," Billy said, shrugging as if it made no difference. "I guess that leaves you only two choices. Wait for a couple of days until the next train leaves, or go on your own dime and allow me to wire your money to the bank at Prescott.''

Longarm didn't like the choices. He much preferred to have government travel and expense money in hand, but he did not wish to wait a few more extra days. After a few moments of deliberation, he reluctantly nodded his agreement.

"But my expense money had better be waiting in Prescott or I'm not giving this Hank Bass a second thought," he warned. "My priority is to find and help my old friend, Jimmy Cox."

"And maybe gain his enduring gratitude and a part of his Spanish treasure?"

Longarm scowled. "That's not the reason I'm skipping New Orleans and you know it."

"Yeah, I do," Billy said, looking contrite. "And I apologize for making the suggestion. It was unfair and I'm ashamed of myself."

"You ought to be," Longarm said, coming to his feet. "All right then, I'll wire you back from Prescott when I've gotten the money and your man."

"Be careful of Hank Bass and watch out for trouble."

"I will," Longarm promised.

Longarm shook Billy's hand and headed for the door. Stopping, he turned to add, "Government expenses should include all rail and stage travel as well as the rental of a good horse for at least three weeks, plus food and lodging. Right?"

"Sure!"

"A hundred dollars will get me started," Longarm decided. "So that's what I'll be expecting when I get to Prescott."

"Consider it already in their bank," Billy told him with a broad, genial smile. "And good luck! I can hardly wait to meet Hank Bass and see him stand before a judge and jury, then be sentenced to the gallows."

"For government mail theft?"

"And for murder, rape, and who knows what else."

"Okay," Longarm said. "You know that I'll try my best to bring him back alive. But I won't pussyfoot around and I'll kill him if he attempts to kill me first or escape."

"He will," Billy promised. "But, if you do that, at

18

least hire a decent photographer to take a picture of his corpse. I'll need one for my files and to satisfy my superiors.''

''Sure thing,'' Longarm called, heading down the now empty federal building hallway.

Chapter 3

Longarm went back to his room and packed for his trip, then hurried over to see a voluptuous young woman by the name of Dolly St. Claire that he wanted to take to dinner and then to bed.

"You're early!" Dolly cried, opening the door and throwing her arms around Longarm's neck while still dressed in only her bra and underpants. "My gawd, you're *really* early!"

Dolly was very strong and she could almost crack a man's neck when she became too exuberant. Longarm had to pry her off and then he stepped back, saying, "I thought we might go somewhere special this evening."

"Sure." Dolly's pretty blue eyes clouded and her full lips formed a childish pout. "On account of your goin' on vacation and not wanting to take me along."

"I'd *like* to take you," Longarm said, not wanting to go over this same contentious ground. "But, as it turns out, I'm not going to New Orleans after all.''

"You're not?!"

"No," Longarm said, shutting and locking the door as his eyes dropped to Dolly's wondrous and bulging breasts. "I'm not. Instead, I have to go to Prescott and then Wickenburg.''

"Never heard of them places."

"They're both in central Arizona.''

"Arizona!" Dolly made a face as if she'd bitten into a lemon. "That doesn't sound like much fun."

"My vacation has been put on hold," Longarm explained. "I'm going to Arizona to help a friend and to capture an outlaw named Hank Bass. I'm told that he's a pretty bad character.''

"What about New Orleans?"

"It will have to wait."

"I wouldn't want to go to Arizona this time of year." Dolly shook her head back and forth. "No sir! Why, it'd be hotter than hell already."

"That's right." Longarm kissed her lips, then whispered, "Maybe I'll take you to New Orleans *next* year."

"You mean it?!"

"No promises, but I'll give it a lot of thought. Have you ever been to the famous French Quarter?''

"No, what is it?"

"It's beautiful," Longarm replied, steering Dolly toward her bedroom. "Lots of old buildings, flowers, wonderful food, music, and people dancing in the street. It's party time all year around in New Orleans's French Quarter, and it's just the kind of place you would love. As pretty as you are, Dolly, you'd be the belle of the ball.''

Dolly cooed happily and didn't even seem to notice when Longarm gently pushed her down on the bed. She

21

closed her eyes and said, "It'd be fun to see something other than Denver. I never been so far from here, you know. Just been to Pike's Peak and a couple of those crummy mining towns up in the Rockies. I envy you for getting paid to go everywhere."

Longarm removed her bra then buried his face in her breasts and began to lick her nipples until they stood at attention.

"Like that?" he asked.

"I'd like to travel," Dolly said dreamily. "Go with you to nice places. Not like that Wickenburg, which sounds pretty awful. But to St. Louis and all those *fun* places."

"This is about to become a 'fun' place right here in your bedroom, Dolly."

She sighed and pressed his face between her creamy mounds of flesh. Longarm felt her body shiver with the first stirrings of passion, but she was fighting hard to keep to the subject of travel.

"I guess I'd go with you to Wickenburg even," she breathed, hands starting to rub his backside. "I mean, if they had a nice hotel where we could make love all the time and a couple of decent places to eat. Do you think that they do, Custis?"

"Huh?"

"In Wickenburg. Do you think they have a nice hotel and eating places? If they do, I'd go there, I guess."

Longarm glanced up at her young, serene face. "No, darling, it's a rough town and you'd hate it."

"Yeah," she said, "I guess I would. But I'll miss you so much."

"Me too," Longarm replied as his hand slipped down and began to ease off her underpants. A few moments later, he jumped to his feet and tore off his own clothes.

"What about that special dinner?" Dolly asked, spreading her legs and giving him a coy smile.

"Just like New Orleans, it'll wait for us."

"Then you *will* take me?"

Longarm gulped and nodded, then he slipped his hands under Dolly's bottom and lifted her, at the same time plunging his big rod into her warm and wet honey pot.

"Ohhh," Dolly groaned as she wrapped her long, shapely legs around his waist and began to slowly drive him insane, "this is a little like having dessert *before* the main dinner course, isn't it?"

Longarm supposed it was. He raised up on his arms and stared down at Dolly, noting how her lips parted and her luscious breasts began to jiggle, keeping time with his vigorous thrusts.

"Can we go soon?" she whispered.

"Yeah," he grunted before lowering his face back into the mounds of her breasts, "we're going real soon."

"Good," Dolly softly moaned, hips moving faster and fingernails starting to dig into his back as her own passion increased. "Oh, good!"

Longarm *liked* this beautiful young woman. Dolly was no genius and she wasn't very sophisticated, but she was clean, honest, and uncomplicated. She didn't ask for much and worked hard at a popular dress shop where she was at her best. It was Dolly's dream to save up enough money to buy her own dress shop, and Longarm had no doubt that someday she'd do it and be extremely successful. On top of that, Dolly was funny and passionate. And a lot of fun to be with, especially in bed.

"Oh, Custis! I'll go *anywhere* with you! Take me to Wickenburg!"

"Can't," Longarm grunted between clenched teeth as

23

the fever in him turned to a fire and he felt himself coming to a thundering climax. "Can't do it!"

Dolly's head began to roll back and forth on the pillow, and their bodies started to lunge at each other as if locked in mortal combat. Longarm raised his head, lips finding her lips as the fire in his testicles spewed like lava through his rod and he began to fill Dolly with great spurts of his hot seed. She cried out with pleasure and stiffened, fingernails raking his back and buttocks as she pulled him down deep into her core, thrashing and thrusting.

They went limp, gasping and clutching, quivering and savoring the last moments of their lusty union.

Later, as they were getting ready to go out and have dinner, Dolly grabbed Longarm's sleeve at the door and said, "You *will* come back and take me to New Orleans, won't you? I mean, you weren't just saying that so you could do it to me again, were you? I would have anyway, you know."

"I know."

Dolly looked so sweet and vulnerable that Longarm gathered her in his arms and said, "I give you my word that I'll take you with me to New Orleans."

She let out a little squeal of delight and about broke his neck again. "You really do mean it this time, don't you?!"

"I do," Longarm said, really meaning it. "We'll just have a hell of a lot of fun. And, besides, you deserve to see something other than Denver and the nearby mining towns. It'd be good to open your eyes to other enjoyable places and experiences."

"I can hardly wait!"

Longarm disengaged himself. "Then we'll do it."

Before he could open the door, Dolly grabbed his hand. "This outlaw that you're going after, is he *really* dangerous?"

"Billy Vail thinks so."

"Please be careful!"

"I always am," Longarm assured her. "So don't worry. Just take care of your own self while I'm gone and dream of the French Quarter."

"I would have thought that was some coin or something," Dolly admitted with a laugh. "Not a place. I mean, a quarter is money, right?"

"Right."

Dolly slipped her arm through his arm, and when they marched down the hall and out onto the street, she turned heads just like always. Longarm felt happy and proud. He wasn't ever going to marry and there was that old friend in Prescott that he was eager to see again, but when he was in Denver, Dolly was his girl and that suited him right down to the ground.

Longarm caught the Denver and Rio Grande the next day, a bit worse for wear due to a strenuous night of lovemaking. No matter, he could sleep on the train and be rested enough when he finally connected with the Santa Fe Railroad that would take him through Albuquerque and then all the way to Ash Fork, Arizona. From Ash Fork, he would probably buy a ticket and ride a stagecoach down to Prescott. Once in Prescott, he'd see what could be immediately done about Hank Bass, then he'd rent a good saddle horse and head for Wickenburg. After that, his plans were completely dependent upon what he found and what the circumstances required.

"Bye-bye!" Dolly called from the railroad platform

25

as Longarm collapsed in his seat beside the window. "Love you!"

Longarm was so pooped that the best he could do was manage a weary smile as the train jerked into a fitful start then rolled south toward Colorado Springs, then Pueblo.

Longarm slept right through Colorado Springs and Pueblo. He didn't wake up until after darkness had fallen on southern Colorado and by then he felt rested and ravenous.

"Porter!" he called to an impeccably uniformed railroad employee.

"Yes, sir?"

"I was wondering if it was too late to get something to eat in the dining car."

"No, sir. Most people have already eaten, but there's a few in there, and you'll have no trouble getting served."

Longarm was relieved at this good news. Knuckling sleep from his eyes and smoothing his clothes, he made his way to the dining car. As promised, it was still half full of passengers, a number of them loudly enjoying a second or even third bottle of wine.

"Evening, sir!" a waiter said in greeting. "Can I take your order?"

"What's the chef's special tonight?"

"Fried chicken, potatoes and gravy, corn on the cob, and French bread, with apple pie for dessert."

"I'll take it."

Longarm was famished and ate nearly an entire loaf of the delicious French bread even before the dinner arrived. Having slept through breakfast and made love with Dolly almost until noon without food, he had some catching up to do.

"You certainly seem to be enjoying your supper," a cultured feminine voice said as he started in on his dessert.

With his fork loaded with pie, Longarm twisted around to see a stylish woman in her mid-thirties eyeing him with more than a passing interest. She was dressed to the nines, with what appeared to be real diamond earrings and a pearl necklace. Her hair was an auburn swirl and her complexion was as clear as African ivory. She was not as young or as beautiful as Dolly St. Claire, but this woman had her own unique appeal.

Longarm lowered his fork. "I guess my table manners aren't the best this evening. Please excuse me for eating like a track layer."

"Oh," she said with a faint smile, "I've always enjoyed watching a hungry man enjoy his food. My father and brothers were farmers, and they ate like starving wolves. Mother was always cooking, and it seemed as if I was always serving food or cleaning in the kitchen."

"You don't look like a farm girl," Longarm remarked, "and I don't mean that to insult your family."

"Then what do you mean?"

He forked the pie into his mouth. "Huh?"

"What does a 'farm girl' look like?"

Longarm knew that she was challenging him and he wasn't about to back down. "Well," he began, "for starters, no farm girl I ever saw wore clothes and jewelry like you're wearing. And they didn't have their hair done up so fine nor have painted fingernails and rouge on their cheeks."

The woman had green eyes and they started to flash, but Longarm headed her off by saying, "And I've never seen one with such a beautiful complexion. I don't mean

27

to be disrespectful, but your skin hasn't seen much sun—it's beautiful.''

His words swept away whatever protest or irritation she might have had and she relaxed. ''My name is Miss Victoria Hathaway.''

''And mine is Custis Long. I'm a United States deputy marshal on my way to Arizona.''

''A federal lawman, how interesting! Now, that *does* surprise me.''

''Why?''

''You look like a successful cattle rancher. Or perhaps an important mining superintendent.''

''Nothing nearly that lofty, miss. But, if you doubt my word, I'd be happy to show you my badge.''

''That's not necessary, Marshal Long. What takes you to Arizona?''

''I have a friend in trouble down near Wickenburg. I mean to help him out, if it isn't too late.''

''Too late for what?''

''To save his life.''

Victoria's eyes widened a little. ''Is he in serious trouble?''

''Probably. He claims to know where to find a Spanish treasure in coin. Jimmy Cox never could keep a secret, and this time it just might have gotten him killed.''

''I hope not!''

''Me too.''

Longarm chose not to say anything about the outlaw Hank Bass because you never knew who might be one of his friends, relatives, or even his lovers. But this elegant and obviously upper-class lady seemed the most unlikely of candidates.

''I'm going to Prescott,'' the woman announced. ''So I guess that we'll be traveling at least partway together.''

"That would please me right down to the soles of my flat feet," he said with a disarming smile. "How are you getting from Ash Fork to Prescott?"

"There will be a buggy waiting."

"Oh."

"One that you'd be welcome to come along in, Marshal."

"Thanks. I'm going to be a little short on funds until the government wires my expense money to Prescott. So your offer is appreciated."

"I'm sure that my fiancé will enjoy meeting you, Marshal Long."

Custis tried hard to mask his disappointment. A fiancé was fine, but he did cut out all the promise of a more interesting relationship. Oh, well, Miss Hathaway was out of his league anyway. And besides, there was that lovely lady friend in Prescott.

Chapter 4

Longarm had an enjoyable train ride to Ash Fork, Arizona, because Victoria Hathaway was fun and a very interesting lady. Over the hundreds of hours they spent together in conversation, Longarm came to know the woman quite well. Victoria really had been a Nebraska farmer's daughter, but had so detested living there and working from morning to night that she had eloped with a traveling salesman when she was just fifteen. Together, they had traveled across the plains and wound up in the Colorado gold fields. Both she and her husband had contracted gold fever and then had made a good strike near Central City.

"And that was when the trouble began between us," she confided. "Art went crazy over the money. Try to imagine that we were literally dressed in rags and down to the last of our food when we struck it rich. Suddenly, we had more money than we knew what to do with and Art couldn't handle it."

"What do you mean?"

"He wanted to buy *everything*! He stayed drunk, spent his nights partying and whoring . . . oh, he just went to hell in a handbasket. I never knew that money could corrupt a man so quickly and completely."

"So," Longarm said, "you divorced Art and took your share of the money?"

"I was going to do that, but he was stabbed to death by a whore and robbed. I wound up with the mine, but legal fees and thieves nearly broke me. Finally, I sold out and took what I had managed to save to Arizona."

"Without a thought of returning to that Nebraska farm country?"

"That's right. I moved to Prescott and bought a nice Victorian house. I opened a cafe—I suppose because of all my experience cooking and doing dishes. The business prospered and I hired someone to manage it, and then immersed myself in civic works which brings you up to my present."

"And your fiancé?"

"He's a banker. Handles all my money and investments. He's older than I am by fifteen years, but we are compatible. Bernard is *very* stable and practical. He would never be corrupted by sudden wealth."

"It sounds like you've come a long way from Nebraska."

"I have," Victoria agreed. "I send money back to my mother. Father died and my oldest brother is running the farm. The rest of my family all moved away—some to California, one to Oregon, but none to Arizona."

"Even so, you're still a relatively young woman. What about children?"

"I don't think that I can have them." Victoria blushed

31

a little. "I mean, it's not as if Art didn't try. Bernard . . . well, he doesn't care for children."

"Do you?"

A deep wistfulness crept into Victoria's eyes. "I'd give *anything* for children. Especially a daughter that I could raise and love."

"Maybe," Longarm suggested, "you ought to think hard about that and consider breaking your engagement."

Victoria gazed out their train window at the passing country. "Believe me," she said, "I've given it some thought."

"I'm sure that there are any number of men who would fall to their knees and beg you to marry them."

"Oh, yes, but probably for my house and money."

"Not so!" Longarm was shocked. Didn't this woman realize how desirable she was in and of herself?

While he was trying to collect the right words to tell her this, Victoria leaned close and said, "What about you? I don't know about such things, but I'm sure that federal marshals, like all other public officials, are underpaid. Lawmen risk their lives for very little monetary compensation."

"That's true enough," Longarm admitted. "We're definitely not in this line of work for the money. On the other hand, we do have a small pension coming—those of us who live to a retirement age."

"Aren't you concerned about being old and poor?"

"No," Longarm said. "I'll never be poor."

"But you don't *know* that. I mean, I don't wish to raise alarm, but a lot of men and women who always thought that something would come around to keep them in their old age do wind up practically on charity."

"I've saved some money and I've invested in some

32

mining stocks that have done just fine. I have a good many friends that owe me a good many favors. Besides all that, I am a pretty simple man and don't require much in the way of material goods or comforts. I have my eye on a piece of mountain property with a cabin in the trees that I could pick up for a song, and I may just do that one of these days.''

Victoria smiled. ''Does it have a stream or river nearby?''

''A river runs right alongside the property. Right now, cottonwood trees are blooming and, in the fall, they will turn gold and red. There are meadows with deer and the fishing is as good as it comes. A rancher friend of mine owns the little homestead and he says that he'll only sell it to me—for a dollar, because he owes me his life.''

''How wonderful!'' Victoria's green eyes had misted. ''I'm so happy that you'll always be taken care of, Custis. We've known each other only a few days, but . . .''

He leaned closer. ''But what?''

Victoria almost kissed him. He could see, even feel her desire, but she was strong and engaged to Bernard, the banker. So she excused herself quite suddenly and went off to powder her face. Longarm took a deep breath. *Steady*, he told himself. *This is no time to fall in love again. Not with Jimmy Cox in big trouble, an outlaw named Bass to arrest and bring to trial, and a promise to Dolly to take her on a vacation in New Orleans. Jezus, Custis, haven't you got enough fires in the iron without getting all worked up over a woman who is engaged to a wealthy banker and has her life completely planned?*

After that, Longarm spent a little more time by himself in the smoking car talking to other men. He and Victoria still had all their meals together, but their relationship had changed and both were aware that their attraction could only end in sadness and disappointment.

And so it was that Longarm and the auburn-haired woman traveled all the way to Ash Fork, each highly aware of the other and each trying to guard their heart.

"Have you ever been to Prescott?" Victoria asked as their train neared Ash Fork.

"Yes," Longarm replied. "Any number of times. But I really can't recall Wickenburg."

"It was once a mining boomtown," Victoria told him. "The reason I know quite a lot about it is that I've gone there often to visit some of my mining investments."

"I see."

"Wickenburg is named after Henry Wickenburg, who founded the town during the Civil War. He was a prospector just poking about in the hills. He had a nasty mule, and one day, in a fit of anger, he picked up a rock and hurled it at the fleeing beast. Turned out that very rock was mostly gold. Wickenburg and some others started up the Vulture Gold Mine, and some brag that it produced more than twenty million dollars before its decline. At one time, Wickenburg was Arizona's third largest city, and it almost became our territorial capital."

"Is that a fact?"

"Only missed it by *two* votes!"

"Fascinating," Longarm murmured, infinitely more interested in Victoria than the history of Wickenburg.

"Why are you staring at me like that?" she asked, blushing.

"I just find you extremely attractive and hope that your Bernard is aware of what a prize he's going to marry."

Victoria's cheeks really did turn crimson now and she looked away, saying, "I'm having second thoughts."

34

"About marrying Bernard?"

"No. About you joining us on the way down to Prescott."

"Why?"

"You're just so . . . so different!"

Longarm reached across the aisle between them and placed a forefinger under her chin. "Look at me, Victoria."

She did.

"What did you expect? I'm a frontier lawman. I live for the hunt and I'm always watching for someone I've arrested or whose brother I might have gunned down and expecting to be ambushed. I have learned to be a loner. I trust very, very few people. I shun permanency and commitments because I am never sure that I'll be around much longer. I prefer the outdoors and . . . yes, even feel most alive when I am in danger."

Longarm leaned back in his seat. "Now, does that sound *anything* like the kind of a fellow who would make a good banker?"

"Absolutely not!"

"Then what *did* you expect?"

"I don't know," she whispered. "I do love Bernard, in a fashion. But I don't find him very . . ."

She couldn't say it, but Longarm thought he knew what she wanted to tell him. He had, over the past few days, picked up enough information about Bernard to draw a mental image of the Prescott banker and investment advisor. Bernard was staid, and considerably overweight, and very, very predictable. He was good, honest, and as boring as a board. He was fussy too. Didn't want children who might interrupt his little routines or disturb his precious serenity. Yes, Longarm knew Bernard. He'd met a few just like him and they bored him to tears.

". . . very exciting," Longarm said, completing her thought. "And, to be honest, Victoria, I doubt you even love the man."

"Love him? I admire and . . . and like Bernard. I'm very *fond* of him."

Longarm wanted to throw up. "What a poor bargain you settle for! And why? Because your heart was broken by your husband and now you prize security and predictability above all other things in a man?"

"Yes!"

"Excuse me," Longarm said, coming to his feet. "But I need some fresh air. I can't stand the thought of you compromising on life. It saddens me, Victoria."

As he was starting to leave, she grabbed his arm. "So what should I do? Fall in love with some penniless lawman who admits, yes, admits that he loves danger?"

"No," Longarm answered. "Marry your banker and become old and safe and bored. You can at least dream of what life should have been like—if you'd only had the courage to live it to the fullest."

Longarm had no more to say to Victoria Hathaway. He was sad, rather than angry, and so, when they finally disembarked at Ash Fork, he didn't even consider riding down to Prescott with her and Bernard. And yes, the banker did prove to be the spitting image of what he'd imagined. The man looked old enough to be Victoria's father, or at least an uncle. He was pudgy, proper, and greeted Victoria with a brotherly peck on the cheek that almost turned Longarm's stomach.

Oh, well, Longarm thought as he headed for the stage line office to make his own travel arrangements to Prescott. *It's her choice and her life—but what a monumental waste!*

Chapter 5

Longarm was reluctant to turn away from Victoria Hathaway, but she'd made her own choices in life and everyone had a right to make mistakes. She, Bernard, and a
tough-looking man who was driving their fine carriage
passed Longarm, and he paused to gaze at her one last
time. Victoria looked right back at him, and he thought
that he detected regret in her pretty eyes.

"Have a happy life!" he called.

Victoria's head turned away, but the driver gave Custis a hard look as they passed on down the street and
out of Ash Fork on their way down to Prescott. With a
sigh of regret, Longarm trudged over to the stage office
and was pleased to learn that his luck was holding and
that the next coach to Prescott would be leaving at mid-
morning.

"Where you from?" the clerk asked, taking Longarm's three dollars.

"Denver."

"Here on business?"

"Yep."

The clerk, a middle-aged man with big muttonchop whiskers and a badly stained brown suit, waited for Longarm to elaborate. When he did not, the clerk said, "You'll be needing a place to stay tonight."

"Yep."

"I'd like to suggest the Majestic Hotel. Clean rooms, good rates. You'll like it."

"What about meals?"

"The Majestic has a dining room. Better than most places to eat in town." The clerk handed him his ticket. "I expect that you are a cattle rancher. Am I right?"

"Nope." Longarm picked up his baggage and started for the door.

"How about a cattle *buyer*?"

"Nope."

"Well, I'll guess it! I most always do by the third try!"

Longarm kept walking out the door. It was to his advantage to keep his true identity a secret—or at least not to advertise himself a federal lawman, because he might just get lucky, step off the stage in Prescott, and accidently bump into Hank Bass. In that case, he'd get the drop on the murderer and arrest him on the spot.

Ash Fork's Majestic Hotel wasn't at all majestic. Instead, the run-down hotel was old and dilapidated with several of the windows boarded over and in desperate need of fresh paint. Longarm took one good look at the place and kept walking. That guy at the stage office was probably getting some kind of payoff for referrals or else one of his relatives owned the Majestic. Either way, Longarm wasn't interested. A half block down the street, he came to a little hotel more to his liking. It was called the Aztec and a sign on the front door advertised: CLEAN ROOMS—FRESH LINEN—NO BODY CRITTERS—ONE DOLLAR A DAY.

"Howdy!" he called, stepping into the hotel and gazing around. It was modest but indeed clean and tidy. The floors were polished and the lobby furniture dusted. Longarm was an expert at sizing up people, weapons, horses, and western hotel rooms. There wasn't a doubt in his mind that this was a well-run establishment.

"Hello there," a respectable-looking woman in her early sixties said, coming out from a back room behind the registration desk. "My name is Ruby and I own this place. Do you need a clean, quiet room for the night?"

"Sure do."

"Be a dollar. Fifty cents more will get you a hot bath, soap, and a clean towel."

"I'll take it."

"You a cattle rancher in town on business?"

"No."

"Railroad executive?"

"Nope." Longarm frowned. "Why is it that everyone keeps trying to guess my line of work?"

Ruby shrugged. "It's mostly because we are bored and there isn't a lot else to do in Ash Fork. We used to have a newspaper, but the editor went broke and left town. So now the only way we can keep track of things hereabouts is to gossip and be nosy. Sorry if it offends you."

"Oh," Longarm said, realizing he was being kind of prickly, "I'm not offended. And I'm not anywhere near as successful as a rancher or railroad executive."

"But you're still not going to tell me what brings you to Ash Fork, are you?"

39

"Nope. And anyway, I'm leaving for Prescott on to-morrow's stage."

"You packing a shooting iron?"

"I am."

"Good! You look like the kind of fella that could handle himself. Might need to, because Hank Bass held up a stagecoach only last week. He gunned down a passenger who was a little slow reaching for his money belt."

"Is that a fact?"

"Yes, it is. So, if you're carrying a bunch of money, you had better be well armed. We've no law in these parts anymore. Never has been any law much to brag about."

"Why not?"

"Hank Bass gunned 'em all down and we can't afford to hire anyone tough enough to stand up to him. Unless someone bushwhacks him or he dies of natural causes, I think we're in for a long, tough time of it."

"Where does Bass mostly hang out?"

The woman chuckled. "Just about anywhere he damn well pleases! Sometimes here, sometimes in Prescott or even Wickenburg. And a lot of the time, he's just *gone*. That's when everyone in this part of the country is happiest. I think he and his boys steal a bunch of money and ride down to Old Mexico where they whoop it up for a couple of months in the cantinas with the pretty young señoritas."

"Why do you think that?"

"Because they always return to Arizona wearing sombreros, serapes, and all kinds of Mexican clothes. They'll gallop in here singing Mexican songs and drinking bottles of tequila."

"That sounds like Old Mexico, all right," Longarm

agreed as he paid for his room and bath, then accepted his key. "Number four, huh?"

"Yeah, anything wrong with that?" Ruby asked.

"Nope. In fact, four is one of my lucky numbers."

"Well," the woman said with a smile, "let's just hope that tomorrow is your lucky day and you don't get robbed on your way down to Prescott."

"I could use a rifle, maybe a shotgun."

"Two doors down on your right is a gun shop. It's owned by an old reprobate named Sherman. He's hard to deal with, but he's fair and he doesn't handle anything but straight shooters. He'll fix you up right."

"Thanks," Longarm said, not telling the woman that he meant to be more than ready for Hank Bass, if the man was unfortunate enough to try to rob him and tomorrow's southbound stage.

The room was as clean as promised and the bathwater was hot. Longarm luxuriated, soaking his travel-weary bones in the tub for nearly an hour before he dried off and climbed into a fresh set of clothes.

He was hungry and so he rang the little bell on the desk. When Ruby appeared, he said, "Where do you suggest I eat?"

"Majestic Hotel has a good dining room. They serve pretty good steaks."

"Place looks dirty to me."

"Oh, it is," Ruby admitted, "but the food is okay. Then again, Antonio's is good for Mexican food and Charley's Platter isn't all bad, if you have a cast-iron stomach."

"I guess I'll try the Majestic's dining room," Longarm said. "Right after I visit the gunsmith and see if I can't buy a good rifle or shotgun."

"He's got what you need," Ruby promised. She

reached down under the counter and pulled out an old but serviceable two-shot .38 caliber derringer. "I bought this little honey from Sherman for just ten dollars."

"Good deal."

"Well, I haven't ever had to use it," Ruby said. "Had to wave it in one fella's face and that was enough to make him decide he ought to pay his rooming bill and get the dickens out of my sight."

"I'm sure it was. Can you hit anything?"

Ruby grinned. "Mister, where you stand right now, I could blow your gizzard out."

"I suspect that you could."

"And I got me a shotgun from Sherman too. Keep it right behind that back door. It's got a barrel as big around as a sweet potato, and there's no doubt it would blow Hank Bass's damned head off."

"Does he stay here?"

"Not anymore, he don't. Used to. But then, that was when he still had some sense and manners. No, sir, the last time he entered this hotel, I grabbed that shotgun, pointed it at his ugly face, and cocked back both hammers."

Longarm raised his eyebrows. "And what happened then?"

"Bass decided to take his business to the Majestic or to the whorehouse, I guess. But he and his boys never came back here, and I don't miss their blood money."

The woman clucked her tongue. "Want to see my shotgun?"

"Maybe another time," Longarm said, heading for the street.

"I'll bet you're a railroad boss! That's what you are! Admit it!" Ruby called.

Longarm had to grin as he strode two doors down and

42

entered the gun shop. Its proprietor, Sherman Hoskins, was a large man with droopy red eyes and a battered face. He was probably in his fifties but looked ten years older. His nose was a red, venous bulb, but his eyes were clear. Longarm pegged Sherman as someone who'd drunk himself into the gutter but then saw the light and pulled himself back from the brink of destruction.

"Howdy," Longarm said to the gunsmith. "I need a rifle or maybe a shotgun."

"Why don't you buy both?" the big man suggested.

"I might do that, if I see what I like and hear a good price," Longarm said, gazing around at the arsenal that Sherman had assembled and placed in gun racks and on pistol pegs.

Longarm took his time checking out the weapons. There was a fine old twelve-gauge double-barreled shotgun made in Germany that he fell in love with but could not really afford. At least, not until he received his expense money from Denver. So he chose a Model center fire 1873 Winchester rifle caliber .44-40 with a skillfully repaired stock.

"Need ammunition?" Sherman asked.

"A couple boxes of shells."

"You got 'em. Where you come from, mister?"

"Denver."

"Where you headed?"

"Prescott."

"Then you really ought to buy this shotgun."

"Can't afford it or I would," Longarm replied. "Maybe on the way back through town."

"Sure," the gunsmith said without enthusiasm. "But I tell you what, if you need a shotgun, I have one in the back room that I can let you have for a measly eight dollars."

"Eight dollars! What kind of a weapon can you sell me that cheap?"

"It's an old double-barrel, ten-gauge. It'll knock you on your ass and you'll think that you've been kicked by a mule, but after it goes off, there won't be nothing standing in the general direction that you pointed."

"Let me see it."

Sherman disappeared for a moment, then returned with the ugly old shotgun. It was scarred and it was heavy, but Longarm could tell the minute that he broke it open that the weapon was in good firing condition.

"Ain't she a cannon, though?" Sherman said, obviously delighted with the weapon.

"That she is," Longarm said. "But I think I'll pass. Too big and heavy."

"You can sell her in a minute down in Prescott for at least fifteen dollars," Sherman argued. "I'll guarantee that you can. And, in the meantime, this shotgun will give you a lot of peace of mind in case you have a chance to blow Hank Bass and his friends all over the sagebrush."

"Yeah," Longarm said. "I see what you mean. All right. How about ammunition?"

"It is hard to come by," Sherman admitted. "But I do have a half dozen shells. Tell you what, I'll throw 'em in for an extra two dollars."

Longarm nodded. Between his stage fare, the Winchester, this shotgun, fresh ammunition, meals and hotel bills, he was getting close to being broke. Billy Vail had damn sure better have his hundred dollars of expense money wired to Prescott, or there was going to be hard times ahead. If worse came to worse, he could point the shotgun at a forest and probably knock down a dozen

44

or so deer along with trees, brush, and anything else that was in his line of fire.

"Thanks," Longarm said, cramming ammunition in his pockets and grabbing the shotgun and the Winchester.

"Come back alive," Sherman said. "And if you want to sell me back them weapons, I'll make you a deal that won't hurt you much."

"I may do that."

"Fact is, I am kind of fond of that old shotgun."

"Then why'd you sell it so cheap?"

"Might blow up in your face," Sherman drawled. "Better you find that out than me."

Longarm *hoped* that the irascible gunsmith was making a little joke—but he wasn't sure.

Chapter 6

When Longarm boarded the stagecoach for the roughly fifty-mile run south to Prescott, he quickly noted that there were *two* guards sitting on top of the stage with rifles.

"Expecting trouble?" Longarm asked the driver.

The man spat a long, brown stream of tobacco juice into the street. "Could happen," he said. "We've got a strongbox full of gold and cash. Hank Bass has spies in Ash Fork so we're taking no chances."

"Good," Longarm said. "As you can see, I'm pretty well armed myself."

"For gawd sakes don't shoot that damned shotgun off or it might blow us all to smithereens!" the driver exclaimed.

"I won't unless I have to," Longarm vowed, tossing his bags into the coach and then clambering inside.

There were only two other passengers, a worried-looking couple in their late sixties who introduced themselves as Mr. and Mrs. George Buelton.

"I'm retired," George said even before Longarm took his seat opposite them. "I was a bartender for over thirty-five years. Hated every gawd damned minute of it. People have a drink, they start to acting like animals. Me and the wife won't touch a drop of the devil's brew."

"We raised four children," Agnes Buelton added. "All of them boys turned out worthless. Just a bunch of drunks, horse thieves, and convicts."

"Real sorry to hear that."

"Not as sorry as we are," Agnes answered. "We're on our way to Prescott so I can be with our daughter-in-law who is having her first baby."

"Well, at least that's a happy occasion."

"Not really," George said glumly. "We can't stand our daughter-in-law, and I doubt that the baby was fathered by our worthless son. He never accomplished a thing in his whole life, and it don't seem possible that he could have pulled this off either."

Longarm turned toward the window. He could already see that this was going to be a long, humorless trip. The Bueltons certainly weren't good traveling company, and he didn't care to hear all the sad details about the failure of their sons or the illegitimacy of their new grandchild.

"You look like a man that has been around some," Agnes said after the coach had left Ash Fork. "You look as if you've had some hard miles."

Longarm was becoming irritated. "Well, ma'am, you don't look that all-fired wonderful to me either."

"What do you do for a living?" George asked, his lips curling down at the corners.

"None of your business."

47

"You might be one of Hank Bass's men gonna pull a gun on us and help him rob this stage."

"You have a better imagination than you have a sense of humor," Longarm clipped with no small amount of sarcasm. "Now, why don't we all just shut up and enjoy the views."

"Seen 'em about a hundred times before," Agnes snapped. "Never seen you before, though."

"And, after we get to Prescott, I don't expect that you ever will again," Longarm said, closing the conversation.

The coach rolled along and the ride was blessedly silent and uneventful all the rest of the way down to Prescott. When it arrived at that scenic and thriving town, Longarm jumped out and marched away, hearing Agnes say, "I still think he's up to no damn good."

"I need a drink," Longarm told the saloon keeper as he dropped his bags and leaned his weapons up against the bar. "Whiskey, and make it a double."

"You just get off the stage from Ash Fork?"

"I did."

"No sign of that poor young woman, huh?"

"What woman?"

"Why, Miss Hathaway. She, her fiancé, and their driver were attacked by Bass and his gang yesterday."

Longarm took a deep, steadying breath. "And?"

"The driver went for his gun and was shot to death. Our banker, Bernard Potter, he was wounded and ain't expected to live. And damned if Bass didn't take Miss Hathaway away. That poor woman hasn't been seen since!"

Longarm tossed his whiskey down. "What about a posse?"

"Ain't nobody willing to ride after that gang."

"Hit me again," Longarm growled.

When he'd had his second drink, Longarm said, "Has this town hired a new marshal?"

"Can't find one stupid enough to take the job," the saloon keeper answered. "Not at *any* price."

"So there's no law whatsoever?"

"Just the law of the gun, same as there is in most towns out west. The dying banker has offered a small dollar reward for the safe return of his fiancée. But he's such a skinflint that a hundred dollars hasn't generated any takers."

"A hundred lousy dollars?"

The saloon keeper shrugged. "What the hell does he care since he's dying?"

"Yeah," Longarm said, "I guess I see your point."

Longarm considered what should be done about Miss Victoria Hathaway. He could not just turn his back on her plight and ride down to Wickenburg to help Jimmy Cox. Not until he put this matter to rest and brought Bass and his men to rope justice.

"Where do you think Bass might have taken Miss Hathaway?"

"Who knows? Most think he took her for ransom. Probably waiting for Mr. Potter to offer a whole lot more than one hundred dollars in reward."

"All right," Longarm said. "Where can I buy or rent a good saddle horse?"

"You going after that reward?"

"Maybe."

"Best forget it," the bartender advised. "A dead man can't spend no piddling hundred dollars of reward money."

"Just answer my question."

"Livery is at the end of the street. Called the Circle

Bar Livery. You can't miss it. The owner, Joe Blue, he won't try to skin you too bad, but he doesn't give anything away either."

"Thanks," Longarm said, picking up his bag, the shotgun, and his Winchester.

"You a bounty hunter?" the bartender shouted as Longarm passed outside.

"Nope."

Several minutes later he was at the livery and talking to Joe Blue, who was slender, as smelly as a billy goat, and about his own age. "Mr. Blue, I need a good horse."

"To buy, or just to rent?"

Longarm frowned, then suddenly remembered that he was almost dead broke. "Be right back," he said. "Got some funds that have been wired to the bank."

"Bank is closed," Blue said. "On account of Mr. Potter being shot up and lyin' on his deathbed."

"When will it reopen?"

"Everybody would sure as hell like to know the answer to that question."

"But I need the money that was wired there to get a horse! And I need it *now*."

"Sorry," Blue said. "I'm real happy to say that I don't have nothin' to do with the bank. I'm smart enough to keep my own money hidden in a tobacco can off somewheres that nobody would ever find."

Longarm dragged out his billfold and counted the last of his personal funds. "I've got . . . thirty-eight dollars left."

"Hell, I'll rent you a horse for that."

"For how long?"

"Depends on which horse."

50

"I'm going after the Bass gang in order to rescue Miss Hathaway."

Blue looked pained. "In that case, you'll have to *buy* a horse, and I can't sell you anything worth anything for no piddling thirty-eight dollars."

"Damn!" Longarm swore in frustration. "There must be *some* way we can work something out. I really need a horse."

"Yeah," Blue said, "but the only way he'll come back is with you draped over his saddle. And most likely, he won't come back at all."

Longarm could see that he wasn't getting anywhere so he started off down the street with his mind in turmoil. Thirty-eight dollars wasn't much but it ought to be enough to buy him some kind of horse. Enough of one to do what needed to be done.

"Hey, mister!" Blue called.

Longarm turned around. "Yeah?"

"I bought a scrub Indian pony yesterday. He's a rank, wicked little son of a bitch, weasel thin and ugly as a possum. But, if you can handle him, he's sound and tough as rawhide."

"What about a saddle, bridle, and blanket? I'm not paying you thirty-eight dollars to ride out of here bareback."

"He came with an Indian saddle and blanket. Ain't nothing more than a pad and some old stirrups on pieces of rope."

"No thanks." Longarm started to walk on, but Blue called out again.

"All right! You win. I'll throw in a decent saddle, bridle, and blanket. Even a pair of saddlebags, halter, lead rope, and a sack of oats."

Longarm suspected that the Indian pony was a real

hellion. Then again, he doubted that he could get a better deal. It was quite likely that Joe Blue had bought the pony dirt cheap and wanted to get rid of him quick.

"Let's see the pony," Longarm growled, coming back to the livery.

"He's out back," Blue said as they walked through the barn to some rickety corrals. "Like I said, he ain't much for looks, but the Indian that sold him to me swore that he was a runnin' fool. Real fast, tough, and sound as a silver dollar."

The moment Longarm's eyes landed on the pony, he knew the horse was an ill-tempered, badly beaten, and mistreated outlaw. The bay gelding was thin, missing part of one ear, and his hide was covered with bald patches where he'd either been bitten by other horses or laid into with a board by his former owner.

"Not a chance," Longarm said, turning to leave.

"Aw, come on! At least give me a chance to show him off to you," the liveryman pleaded. "I'll ride him first. Then you can ride him and I'll make you a hell of a deal."

"How much?"

"Thirty dollars with everything included."

"Twenty."

"Hell no! The saddle is worth near that much!"

"Then shoot the little bugger and sell the saddle to someone else," Longarm announced as he picked up his bags and prepared to walk away.

"Twenty-five for everything and I'll throw in a quirt and pair of spurs. You'll need 'em."

Longarm thought, What the hell. If he could ride the pony and leave Prescott with thirteen dollars still resting in his pockets, he'd be getting off very well indeed. It was, he decided, at least worth a try.

"Tell you what, Joe. Go ahead and saddle him up and let's see what he can do."

The liveryman gulped. "All right. But he don't much care for people so it may take a few minutes. You could come back in say . . . oh, an hour."

"I'll stay and watch."

It *did* take an entire hour for Joe Blue to rope then subdue the fighting pony and get him saddled. When he mounted the gelding, it didn't buck but instead charged out of the corral like its tail was on fire. The Indian pony raced up the street, scattering pedestrians in every direction like a flock of squawking chickens.

Longarm almost laughed out loud, but he did have to admit that the pony was very fast. Fifteen minutes later, Joe Blue came storming back down the street. Longarm was astonished to see that the pony was barely winded.

"See! I told you he was fast and sound!"

"And out of control. No thanks."

"Twenty dollars! Please!"

"All right," Longarm finally agreed. "If you will throw in a couple of rifle scabbards."

"What?!"

"Just fix me up something out of a gunnysack or a piece of canvas to carry this rifle and my big shotgun."

"Damn, you are tough to deal with! I'm losing my ass on this deal."

"I doubt it," Longarm replied without a shred of sympathy. "You probably bought this pony for a jug of whiskey. Has it a name?"

"I call him an ornery son of a bitch. You can call him anything you want."

"I'll call him Cyclone," Longarm decided, reaching for his wallet and counting out twenty dollars. As he handed over the money, he wondered if he'd just made a very bad mistake. After tying his weapons and giving Cyclone a drink of water, he said to Joe Blue, "Were you me, where would you start to find Bass and that poor Hathaway woman?"

"I wouldn't. No use in making *two* bad mistakes in the same day," Blue said, pocketing Longarm's money.

"I'm serious. Someone has to rescue Miss Hathaway."

"She's worth more alive than dead," Blue reckoned aloud. "Bernard Potter has a bank full of cash and he'll pay her ransom."

"Yeah," Longarm said, "but then they might decide to keep or kill her anyway."

"Keep her for what?"

"She's a beautiful woman, or haven't you ever noticed?"

"Yeah, I noticed," Blue said. "And I expect that you are right. As for finding Bass and his boys, I know that they have a cabin southwest of town about thirty miles. There's a big lightnin' struck tree by a fork in the road leading up to that cabin. It sits under some high red rocks at the back of a little canyon."

"I guess that I can find it."

"Be better if you didn't, and I can't say for sure that is where they took the woman. But it makes sense. They wouldn't have gone back to Mexico without getting a ransom. From what I hear, they got less than a hundred dollars off the banker before they shot him in the gut."

"I hope he lives," Longarm said.

"Not me. I owe him two hundred dollars."

Longarm didn't have a reply to that remark, so he had Blue hold Cyclone by the bit and then he climbed on, jammed his boots deep in the stirrups, grabbed the saddle horn, and said, "Point him in the right direction and get out of our way."

The moment that Joe Blue released Cyclone, the pony jumped forward and took off like a bat out of hell. Longarm didn't release the saddle horn until the pony finally became winded about three miles south of town.

"Well," Longarm said, pulling the horse down to a trot, "I hope that you've run the piss and vinegar out of your system and that we can settle down and be friends. If you help me to save Miss Hathaway, I'll turn you loose so that you can run free with mustangs."

Cyclone laid his ears back and Longarm doubted that he understood, but that didn't matter. He was going to keep the Indian pony moving until he reached Bass's cabin in the trees and, after that, he wouldn't need Cyclone anymore anyway.

Chapter 7

Longarm had a lot weighing on his mind as he rode southwest in search of Victoria Hathaway and the Bass gang. He was none too happy about having to ride an outlaw pony and wondered if he would ever get his federal money, which would have been wired and forwarded to Bernard Potter's now shuttered bank.

Oh, well, he would worry about that later. The main thing now was to locate this cabin, sneak in, and then get the drop on Hank Bass and his bunch of cutthroats. Longarm chided himself for not taking the time to find out more about the Bass gang. For example, it would have been helpful to know how many men had been in on yesterday's shootings and abduction.

It was almost sundown before he reached a fork in the road and noted a large, lightning-torched tree. Longarm gazed up a narrow, red-rocked canyon. Yes, this was where he ought to find the Bass gang. They were so brazen that they hadn't even posted a sentry to guard the mouth of the canyon.

Being on the cautious side, Longarm reined the pony into a draw and then dismounted. He tied Cyclone to a tree and then decided to take both the Winchester and the heavy but very intimidating shotgun.

"Cyclone," he warned, "don't even think about whinnying or breaking free."

In answer, Cyclone attempted to take a bite of his shoulder, but Longarm was too quick and managed to jump beyond the range of the pony's snapping teeth.

"Dammit, I *may* put you out of your misery when this is over," Longarm swore. "You just better hope these outlaws plug me before I plug them."

Longarm felt a little better having given the pony a piece of his mind. He checked his weapons and then began to move toward the canyon, staying low and following a dry wash that would hide his approach. The wash was heavily choked with creosote bushes and sagebrush, and it seemed to lead all the way up into the canyon. Birds flitted through the heavy shrubs, and Longarm almost stepped on a brightly colored Gila monster that opened its big jaws and slowly backed away.

He might not have even seen the guard posted up on the side of the canyon if the man hadn't lit a cigarette just as dusk fell. Longarm dropped flat and gazed up at the sentry. The man was about two hundred yards away and the fool was clearly bored to death. He was just sitting on a rock, gazing out toward the first colors of the sunset. But it would be a climb to reach him, and Longarm knew that plenty could go wrong. If he dislodged a rock, the guard would probably hear it move and then Longarm would be at a serious disadvantage being downslope and out in the open.

There was really no help for it, though. Longarm sleeved sweat from his brow and settled down to wait for complete darkness to shroud the canyon. He stretched out on a big flat rock, leaned his weapons against a bush, and admired the Arizona sunset, thinking that there were few better than the ones you got to enjoy in this southwestern territory. As for any kind of plan to rescue Miss Hathaway, he didn't give it much of a thought. Longarm had found over the years that advance planning in cases where you had no idea what to expect was most generally a waste of mental effort.

The first thing to do was to eliminate the guard up on the canyon wall. After that, he would sneak along the rim of the canyon, locate the cabin, and make his way down to it sometime after midnight when the outlaws were almost certain to be asleep. If all went well, he could get the drop on them and that would be the end of this business. However, even if everything went wrong, he had the huge scattergun; the only thing he had to really worry about was not blowing Miss Hathaway to smithereens along with Hank Bass and the rest of his gang.

When the sunset finally played out and the sky grew dark, Longarm tugged down his hat, picked up the shotgun and rifle, then started climbing. Every nerve was tingling and he was very careful where he placed his feet, but after about fifteen minutes he stopped and heard snoring.

"Thanks," he said, glancing up at the stars as he relaxed and climbed the rest of the way to the rim. There was plenty of moonlight to see the guard; the man was fast asleep. Longarm set his weapons down, unholstered his gun, and then pistol-whipped the sentry hard enough to make sure that he did not awaken for at least twelve hours.

"Consider yourself the lucky one this night," Longarm said, leaving the unconscious sentry.

He only had to hike about a half mile before he saw a little one-room cabin. The outlaws were sitting outdoors around a blazing campfire. Longarm counted four. He tried but was unable to identify Victoria Hathaway and decided that she might be locked in the cabin.

"So what do you do now?" he asked himself. "Wait until late like you planned, or circle down in behind that cabin and try to sneak inside and rescue the woman? If you could get her out of harm's way, then you'd have a hell of a lot less to worry about."

That approach made a lot of sense to Longarm. His main objective was to get the woman to safety. After that, he would deal with the Bass gang. And frankly, with the old ten-gauge double-barreled shotgun coupled with the all-important element of surprise, Longarm figured the odds were yet in his favor.

He hiked about a mile before finding a good trail that would take him down behind the cabin. Thanks to the moonlight, it wasn't too difficult, and Longarm could plainly hear outlaw laughter. Once, he thought he also heard Victoria's voice crying out from the cabin, but he was not certain until he reached its back wall and then heard her sobs and the lusting grunts of one of the outlaws. There was a window but it was caked with dust. Longarm used the sleeve of his coat to rub a little clearing in the window so that he could look inside. A candle flickered but it gave off enough light so that Longarm could see one of the outlaws rutting on top of Victoria. The pig hadn't even bothered to remove his pants but had instead just dragged them down around his boot tops

59

and was now completely lost in his passion.

Rage filled Longarm and he moved swiftly around to the corner of the cabin. The campfire was only about thirty feet from the front door, but Longarm knew he had no choice but to try to get inside. Taking a deep breath and knowing that he could not handle both the Winchester and the shotgun at the same time, Longarm placed his rifle down, then slipped around the corner and into the cabin, almost certain that he would have to shoot the outlaw and then fight his way back outside.

The outlaw was still lost in his passion. Grunting and thrusting powerfully into poor Victoria, he would not have heard a train had it roared right through the cabin. All that Longarm had to do was walk over to the bed and mash his brains with the heavy butt of his shotgun. The man's entire body quivered and stiffened, then he went limp. Longarm knew that he had killed this one and it didn't bother him in the least. He grabbed the man by the back of his dirty shirt and dragged him off Victoria Hathaway, then bent down and clamped his hand over her mouth before she could even think about screaming.

"Victoria," he whispered, "it's me! Marshal Custis Long. Do you understand?"

The young woman was so battered and shaken that she attempted to claw his eyes out. Longarm had quite a struggle before he got her calmed down enough to think straight.

"Victoria, I'm sorry," he whispered, leaning close to her ear. "These dirty sons a bitches are going to pay for this, I swear they will! But you've got to do as I say or we both may die. There's still four outside."

She began to cry again and hugged his neck with all of her strength. Longarm wanted to comfort her, but there wasn't time. Another outlaw might come in for his turn at any moment.

"Victoria," he said, holding her tight, "what happened here isn't your fault—it's their's and they're going to pay for it with their lives. But I need you out of harm's way before the shooting starts. Do you understand me?"

"Yes," she said in a hushed voice. "Can *I* kill them too?"

"No. I want you to try and get out of here. If I am killed, there is a trail behind this cabin that leads up to the canyon's rim. Once on top, head down canyon and you'll discover an unconscious guard. Take his weapons and then keep moving as fast as you can. About a mile away, you'll find my pony. Ride him back to Prescott."

"I can't leave you!"

Longarm felt her fingernails bite into his shoulder. "Please! Let me stay and help! I *owe* them!"

There was so much venom and anger in the woman's voice that Longarm didn't have the heart to deny her wish. "All right. Here," he said, helping Victoria dress before handing her the rifle and saying, "I need to know—have you ever fired one of these before?"

"You bet I have!"

"Good. It's loaded and ready for action. Just aim and pull the trigger."

"I'm going to kill Hank Bass!"

Longarm went back to the cabin door and pushed it open a crack. "Can you point him out for me?"

Victoria would have collapsed on her way to the door if Longarm hadn't caught and supported her. Easing it open a crack, he said, "Which one is he?"

She stared for several moments, then said, "I . . . I don't think that he's out there!"

61

"Are you sure?"

Victoria looked again. "Yes," she said in a dead voice. "He's not among them."

"Where could he have gone?"

"I don't know. Maybe just to check the horses or . . . or relieve himself."

"We'll wait a few minutes," Longarm decided. "I don't want him to come barging in and put a bullet through us."

Victoria sagged against Longarm's chest, and he could feel her shaking. He held her close and smoothed her hair.

"How is Bernard?" she asked when she could get the words out.

"He's a goner," Longarm had to tell her. "The bank is closed and everyone is upset."

Victoria began to cry, so Longarm held her even tighter. "Are you sure you don't want to try and get out of here before the fireworks?"

"No!"

"Then you've got to get a grip on yourself," Longarm told her. "Just as soon as Hank Bass rejoins those men, we're going to end their little party once and for all. And no matter what, if they won't surrender, I'm going to shoot Bass first."

But even as Longarm was making this solemn pledge, one of the outlaws came to his feet, glanced at the cabin door, and then rubbed his crotch in a way that caused the others to burst into coarse laughter.

"Think I've got another itch for that woman that I'm going to take care of right now!"

Longarm stepped in front of Victoria and his words were deadly. "I don't think so, you raping son of a bitch!"

The man's jaw dropped in amazement, and he was ridiculously slow in making a stab for his gun. Longarm pulled one of the triggers of the shotgun and it exploded like a Civil War cannon. The outlaw with the "itch" was lifted completely off the ground and nearly torn apart by the blast. Longarm shifted the barrels and fired again, and two more of the outlaws were knocked down like wheat in a high wind.

Victoria shot the last one. Her rifle thundered and the man took the bullet in the groin. He screamed, grabbed himself, and then began to writhe around in the dirt. Longarm knew that the man didn't have a chance of surviving the wound. He hurried over to him, knelt on one knee, and shouted, "Where's Bass?!"

The dying outlaw tried to speak but instead died in a pool of his own blood.

A bullet out of the dark clipped Longarm's rib cage, and he spun around just in time to see a mounted horseman fire again before galloping away.

"That's Hank Bass!" Victoria cried.

Longarm ran to the corral, and the already spooky horses began to mill about in fear. They could probably smell the gunpowder and blood and associated it with past frightening experiences.

"Whoa!" Longarm called.

But the outlaw horses were crazed and nearly trampled Longarm as they bolted through the open gate and went flying down the canyon after Hank Bass.

"Dammit!" Longarm shouted in angry frustration before getting a hold of himself and realizing that, even though Hank Bass had escaped, everything had turned out quite well. Hank Bass might still be free, but now he was alone and on the run.

•   •   •

Longarm dragged the bodies into the cabin and found some blankets. He wrapped Victoria up like a baby and held her close. Neither of them slept a wink, but when the sun finally peeked over the canyon's rim, Longarm was pleased to see that the young woman was composed.

"What are we going to do now?" Victoria asked.

"I'll inspect the cabin for any bounty that they haven't yet spent in Mexico," he replied. "After that, I'll just set the damn thing on fire and cremate the lot of them."

"You can do that?"

"There's no law in Prescott that could take over the case, and I doubt that any citizens would want to come clear down here and bury these men out of the kindness of their hearts."

"Yeah," she said, taking Longarm's hand, then gazing up into his eyes and saying, "I thought a lot about you last night, Custis. I owe you my life but . . ."

Victoria broke down and began to cry, so Longarm put his arms around her awhile until she regained her composure. "What's wrong?" he asked.

"Everyone will know what these *animals* did to me."

"Oh, I don't know if . . ."

"Yes, they will! And, if there were any doubts, Bass will brag and tell them."

Longarm supposed she was right. Most everyone would assume that a pretty young woman abducted by a band of cutthroats and outlaws would most likely be violated in the most unspeakable manner. Imaginations would run wild.

"What am I going to do, Custis?!"

"You're going to have to be very strong," he said, knowing how feeble this advice would sound but unable to think of anything better to say. "You did *nothing* wrong. If there is sin, it's on *their* unholy souls, not yours.''

She nodded, chin quivering. "But . . ."

"Victoria," he interrupted, "I don't know you real well, but we became quite close on the train, didn't we?"

"Very close."

"Then my advice would be that, unless you have some compelling reason to remain in Prescott, you should relocate. Just go someplace new and give yourself a little time and space to heal. Maybe you'll come back, but maybe not. Either way, time will heal."

"You sound like a man who speaks from experience."

"I do," he said, not wishing to elaborate on the many sorrows in his own past.

Victoria was quiet for a time and then she said, "Could we get this over with and leave this evil place?"

"Sure." Longarm left her by their dying campfire and went into the cabin. He searched it thoroughly and did find a big coffee can filled with stolen money and jewelry. Taking it outside, he said, "Hold this while I finish up this foul business."

He went back inside and found matches, then dropped them on the floor and the bed. The straw mattress erupted in flames and Longarm hurried outside. This wasn't being done strictly according to the law book, but there was no reason for an inquest or to waste good taxpayer time and money giving scum like those inside a proper burial. And if some do-gooder objected, he or she could collect their charred bones and inter them in a grave and have a little ceremony. But they'd do so at their time and expense.

When the fire was raging, Longarm took Victoria's

arm and they walked slowly back down the canyon. When they reached its mouth, they turned north toward Prescott.

"I almost hope that Hank Bass spotted my horse," he remarked as they trudged along.

"But why?! If that happened last night, we'll be afoot."

"Yeah," Longarm conceded, "but there is also a fair chance that Cyclone just might have either stomped or bitten him to death."

Victoria looked up at him with a curious expression, so Longarm added, "When you see Cyclone, you'll understand."

"Oh."

Victoria said nothing more until they climbed down in a gully and saw that the ugly little pony was still alive and waiting.

"Stand back," Longarm warned, dodging a hoof and then leaping forward to grab Cyclone by the halter and twist his ear until the pony quivered with pain. "Now, get on his back!"

"Are you—"

"Hurry!"

Victoria climbed into the saddle, and Longarm released Cyclone's ear and then swung up behind her. He grabbed the reins and then he gave the little bay demon its head. As always, Cyclone took off running like a scalded cat, heading straight south for Wickenburg.

Chapter 8

By the time that Longarm and Victoria rode double into Wickenburg, the hour was growing late and even Cyclone was stumbling with weariness.

"I'll get us rooms at the Trevor House," Longarm said as he helped Victoria down. "Would you also like me to summon a doctor?"

"Heavens no!"

"Are you sure?" Longarm asked, knowing full well the savagery that Victoria must have endured at the hands of the Bass gang.

"Yes," she said, straightening her dress. "What I really want is a hot bath, a bottle of cognac, and a good night's sleep. This whole thing has been a nightmare."

"You're going to have to talk about it to someone," Longarm told her. "You have any close lady friends in Wickenburg?"

"I do . . . and I will." Victoria started to turn away. "And, Custis?"

67

"Yes?"

"Are you sure that Bernard is dead?"

"No. But I would imagine so."

"And he *only* offered a hundred dollars reward for my safe return?"

Longarm heard the now familiar tremor in Victoria's voice. "I'm sure that he offered much more. Don't dwell on it. I'll ask around about your fiancé and, if no one knows his condition, we'll wire Prescott first thing in the morning."

"Thank you. Will you be coming in soon?"

"Yeah," Longarm said. "But first, I need to get some answers of my own."

"About that old prospector friend, Jimmy Cox?"

"That's right. And about Hank Bass. He may have come here after he escaped the canyon last night. I'd say there's a reasonable chance that he might even be found drowning his sorrows in one of the local watering holes."

"You be very careful."

"I will," Longarm said. "And there's the matter of this money that we found in the cabin. I'm going to put it in the bank tomorrow morning after I deduct some travel money. I'll let someone else sort things out later."

Victoria studied Cyclone. "He really did quite well, you know."

"He's an outlaw," Longarm said. "But I did promise to give him his freedom if he behaved."

"You're turning him loose?"

"Damn right I am," Longarm said. "Best thing to do before he kills someone."

Longarm did exactly what he'd promised. After leaving Victoria in front of the hotel, he rode the ill-tempered but bighearted Cyclone out to the end of town, unsaddled then unbridled him and set him free. The pony surprised him by not immediately bolting away in a dead run. It turned its ugly head and stared at him in the moonlight, as if asking what would happen next.

"You're free! Get the hell out of here and stay away from anything that walks on two legs."

Cyclone snorted and then wheeled about to vanish into the deepening night. Longarm knew that he would never see the little outlaw again and that was just fine.

The saloons were full and roaring. Longarm had always found them to be excellent sources of information. Also, he felt in need of strong spirits, but not too strong just in case he really did run into Hank Bass. But that would be too easy and, so far, nothing on this trip was turning out easy. What Longarm most wanted to know was the whereabouts of Jimmy Cox. And that's why, after tossing his saddle, bridle, and blanket just inside the door of the Sawdust Saloon, he headed straight for the bar and sidled up against a wizened old prospector.

"Evening," Longarm said with a disarming smile. "Can I buy you a drink?"

The prospector eyed him suspiciously. "Now, why in the hell would you want to do that?"

"Maybe I don't like to drink alone."

"And maybe you're stuffed full of horseshit," the prospector said.

"Yeah," Longarm admitted, "maybe some of that too. I'd still like to buy you a drink and take a load off my feet."

"Then buy us a *bottle*," the old prospector said. "That way, we won't have to keep getting up for refills. And, at the same time, I promise that I'll be the best damn listener you ever drank with."

Longarm almost laughed. He ordered a bottle of whiskey and then led the way through the saloon's noisy crowd to an empty table near the back of the room. He took a seat with his back to the wall where he could keep an eye on things.

"My name is Custis," he said, uncorking the bottle, then filling two glasses.

"Name is Eli," the prospector replied as he raised his glass. "And I *do* like whiskey! Even bad whiskey."

Longarm returned the token salute and they emptied their glasses. The whiskey was dreadful but Longarm managed to keep from choking, although his eyes began to water and it felt like he'd swallowed a shovelful of sulfur.

"Whew!" Eli breathed. "This is sure to take away all a man's woes."

"For a while at least," Longarm agreed. "I take it that you are a prospector."

"Yep. And if you're looking for someone to grub-stake, you couldn't do better'n me. I been roamin' around this miserable desert country for almost thirty years. Keepin' one step ahead of the Apache and findin' more'n my fair share of gold."

"Is that a fact?"

"It is!" Eli shouted, vigorously nodding his head up and down. The wrinkled old prospector emptied his glass, then refilled it to the brim, leaning forward to whisper, "And I have made men smart enough to stake me *rich*."

"For a fact?" Longarm asked, pretending to look very impressed.

"That's right! And you could be the next."

Eli winked and took a long draft from his glass. "But I'll be honest with you, there are no guarantees. I might hit another pocket of gold on my first day out . . . or it could take months.''

"I understand.'' Longarm took another drink. "What about finding me some *Spanish* gold?''

Eli had started to raise his glass, but now he thumped it down hard. "Ain't no damned Spanish gold! Are you just another one of them greedy sons a bitches that read that newspaper article about the old liar, Jimmy Cox?''

"I did,'' Longarm decided to admit. "The article said that Jimmy paid off his debts with Spanish coins.''

"So what?!'' Eli shouted loud enough to turn heads. "You want to know the truth behind that story?''

"Sure.'' Longarm poured Eli another two fingers of the awful whiskey and leaned back in his chair.

"Well, Jimmy Cox is a friend of mine and . . . while he's a good man, he's also a *terrible* liar.''

"Is that a fact?''

"It is! He had fallen on real hard times. Couldn't get nobody to grubstake him 'cause he hadn't found so much as a thimbleful of gold for years. So what does he up and do?''

"I don't know. You tell me.''

"He concocts this crazy story about finding Spanish gold!''

"But there are plenty of witnesses who say that he paid all his medical bills with Spanish gold coins.''

"Yeah, yeah, but . . . well, I expect he found 'em down in Mexico or something and just hoarded enough of 'em over the years so that he could cause a stir.'' Eli wagged his head back and forth. "It was all a *hoax*! And damned if it probably didn't get old Jimmy killed.''

Longarm leaned forward over the table. "So you think he's dead?''

"I don't know,'' Eli admitted. "No one has seen

Jimmy for months. But old desert dogs like us can disappear for long periods of time so . . . well, it's hard to say if he is alive or dead. All I do know for sure is that a lot of greedy sons a bitches are hunting for him. And, if he was found, then I'm sure they must have tortured Jimmy for the location of that Spanish treasure. He'd either have had to tell them or else.''

"Or else what?''

"Or else they'd have killed him. I expect that they probably did either way.''

Longarm emptied his glass. "I'm an old friend of Jimmy's,'' he admitted.

"Sure you are!''

"No, it's true! Jimmy saved my life a few years ago, and I've come to try and return the favor.''

"Well,'' Eli said, "I expect that you are way late. Like I said, Jimmy was havin' hard times, and I believe he just made up the whole story. Could be he even got someone to give him those Spanish coins so they could work the local folks into a frenzy and start another gold rush. That kind of thing does a lot for the local businessmen, you know.''

"I see your point,'' Longarm said, "but it just doesn't sound like the kind of thing that Jimmy Cox would do. I mean, his word was his bond. He was a little crazy and difficult to be around sometimes, but he wasn't the kind to pull off that type of complicated hoax.''

Eli shrugged. "Then someone else talked him into it. I dunno. But I'll guarantee you it *was* a hoax and one that I figure backfired and got old Jimmy plugged.''

"Help me to find him,'' Longarm whispered. "Help me to get to the bottom of his disappearance.''

"No,'' Eli said, grabbing the bottle and starting to rise. "It's too damn dangerous.''

Longarm clamped his hand on the prospector's wrist. "I *need* your help and I'm willing to pay for it."

Eli relaxed, then slumped back down in his chair. "So," he said, "you do have money. What are you, a rancher or someone important?"

"No," Longarm said. "Anyway, the reasons why I want to find Jimmy are good and they don't include murdering him for some Spanish coins. I really do owe the man my life, and I mean to repay him at any cost."

"I need a good grubstake," Eli said. "A *real* good grubstake."

"Which would cost?"

"About a hundred dollars ought to be enough."

"I've got that much money being wired to me from Denver," Longarm said. "Thing of it is, the money was sent to Prescott and is probably resting in the bank."

"So, we can go get it!"

"Maybe," Longarm said, not wishing to go into the business of the Prescott bank's being closed because of a death. Better, he decided, to just use some of the recovered cash he'd gotten before torching the Bass gang's cabin.

"Listen, Eli, I'll get the money somehow. The thing that's important is that you have some idea of where to start looking for my friend. It's big country out there, and I don't have any time to waste."

"I have a fair idea where he was heading when he left town the last time," Eli admitted.

"Good! Then we can leave tomorrow."

"We can leave when you get your money and grubstake us," Eli corrected. "Tomorrow, or the next day, or the next, it don't matter to me."

"Well," Longarm said, "it matters to me. Jimmy Cox may be suffering torture right now."

"Or singing with a harp in heaven or howling in hell," Eli added.

"Yeah, that too," Longarm replied. "Tomorrow then?"

"You leavin' me with this bottle still half full?"

"I am," Longarm said. "I'm leaving while I've still got a stomach and I suggest that you do the same."

Eli chuckled. "I been drinkin' this and worse for forty years and I'm healthy as a horse. Guess that I'll finish this bottle."

"I'll get the money and meet you here tomorrow morning," Longarm told the man. "Just be sober enough to buy what we need and leave."

"You got a horse?"

"No."

"Good," Eli said. "We'll walk. Better buy yourself some extra heavy boots."

"No," Longarm said, "*you* walk if that's your style. I'm buying or renting a horse."

"Suit yourself, but he'll have a damned hard go of it out there on the desert without food nor water."

Longarm scowled. Maybe, he thought, he had better forget about a horse after all. "How far do you think we'll have to go to find Jimmy?"

"He'll be within fifty miles, one way or the other."

This news did not comfort Longarm. "All right, Eli. But if you're leading me on a dead-end trail, you're going to be real damned sorry."

The prospector cackled softly as he poured another drink. "Mister," he said, "I've *always* been sorry. I'll die sorry. Don't matter to me, though, as long as I die rich."

Longarm left the man. He collected his old saddle, blanket, and bridle at the door and visited a couple more saloons, asking if anyone had seen Hank Bass. No one had, so he wearily returned to his hotel room.

He slept long and well that night. When he awakened, Longarm dressed, shaved, and went to the telegraph office to find out about the condition of Victoria's fiancé.

"Mr. Potter died of his gunshot wounds yesterday," the telegraph operator announced. "There's a funeral tomorrow morning in Prescott at ten o'clock."

"I see. Has his bank been reopened?"

"Now that I do not know."

"Thanks." Longarm had a big breakfast and then returned to his hotel to say good-bye to Victoria.

"Will you be back soon?" she asked, looking pale and shaken over the news of Bernard's death.

"I don't know," Longarm replied. "But I will return. I've still got Hank Bass to catch or kill."

Victoria lifted up on her toes. "You take good care of yourself."

"I'll try," Longarm told her.

"I'll be waiting for you to return, Custis. And . . . and I'll never be able to repay you for saving me up in that canyon."

Longarm grinned. "It was my pleasure. Just wish we could have made it a clean sweep. You take care, now."

"Sure," she replied.

Longarm left Victoria and went to hunt up Eli. He figured that his best chance of finding the old prospector was in the saloon where he'd left the man last night, and so that was where he began his search. But Eli wasn't there nor was he in any of the other saloons.

Longarm went hunting in the hotels and even the livery, but Eli was nowhere to be found. At least, not until he heard a man shout and emerge from an alley yelling, "Old Eli is dead! Someone cut his throat!"

Longarm bolted forward and rounded a building on a dead run. He sprinted up the alley and skidded to a halt beside Eli's stiff corpse. Someone had cut the poor old bugger's throat from ear to ear.

"Jezus!" a man croaked with revulsion. "Old Eli never had any money. Now, who in the world would do such a terrible thing?!"

"I don't know," Longarm said in a hard, flat voice, "but before I leave this country, I damn sure mean to find out."

Chapter 9

Longarm couldn't say for certain whether he was connected to Eli's death or not. All he knew for sure was that the old prospector had met a very sad and violent end while Longarm's own hopes of unraveling the mystery of Jimmy Cox had taken a major setback.

So what was he to do now? That afternoon, they had a funeral procession down the main street and Longarm followed it out to the cemetery. There weren't a lot of people in attendance, mostly prospectors and town drunks, but it was clear that they had all been Eli's good friends. One old codger, tall, proud looking, and in his sixties with a long, flowing white beard, seemed to be especially affected by Eli's death. When Eli was placed in his grave, it was this man who took a Bible out of his coat pocket, smoothed it in his big hands, and then spoke for everyone.

"As you know," he began, head bowed and hat in

hand, "Eli Jones was my very best friend. I've lost *two* best friends lately, Eli and Jimmy Cox, who we all know is probably deader'n a doornail. And I don't know how God can have 'em end up so badly, but I sure do want to ask Him to welcome their departed souls."

The man took a deep, shuddering breath, then continued, "Ain't none us nothin' but terrible sinners, Lord. You know that we all are. But, Lord, we ain't the kind of son of a bitch that cut poor Eli's throat or did away with Jimmy. Sure, we'll whore and get drunk every chance we have, but we ain't killers and none of us would ever hurt anyone out of spite or pleasure."

"Amen!" another miner shouted. "Tell it sweet, Preacher Dan!"

"And so, Lord, take poor Eli's soul to Your bosom and give him comfort in Your heaven. Give him good whiskey and meat, and some gold to fill his pockets. That's all any one of us could ask of You, Father in heaven. Amen."

Longarm was just as touched by the short but sincere sermon as anyone in attendance. And when a hat was passed around to cover the cost of Eli's funeral, he contributed generously from the money he'd found hidden in Bass's canyon cabin. Afterward, everyone trudged back to Wickenburg and proceeded to get roaring drunk. Everyone, that is, except for Preacher Dan, who lingered at the cemetery.

Not wishing to intrude, Longarm waited until the impressive old preacher returned to town and then intercepted him. "Excuse me, Preacher Dan," he began, "but I'd like a word with you."

The preacher stopped, and Longarm could see that his eyes were red from weeping. He had wide shoulders and must have been a fine specimen of manhood in his youth, but now those broad shoulders sagged with defeat and too many hard years.

"What do you want?" the preacher asked in a voice raspy with emotion.

"I need your help," Longarm said.

"I don't understand."

Longarm reached into his pocket and dragged out his federal badge. "I'm a United States deputy marshal and my name is Custis Long. I came all the way from Denver to arrest Hank Bass and to find out what happened to my old friend Jimmy Cox. Last night, I made a bargain with Eli, who agreed to help me find Jimmy."

The preacher stared at the badge in Longarm's fist. He took a deep, ragged breath and asked, "What has this to do with me?"

"You said that Jimmy Cox was your other best friend. I thought, given that two of them are gone, you might want to help me find out who killed them. I can't do it without your help, Preacher."

The big man had ice-blue eyes, so sad that Longarm wondered what awful suffering he had endured in this world.

"Marshal, I'm very sorry, but I can't help you," he finally decided aloud.

"If you don't, Eli's murderer will never be found. You see, I'm pretty sure he was killed because someone learned that he was going to help me find Jimmy Cox."

"I doubt that."

"The man was *broke*," Longarm said. "He had nothing to steal. As far as I could tell, the only thing he had of value was the knowledge of where to start looking for Jimmy."

"Pure speculation, Marshal."

"When it comes to murder, I'm a good speculator, Preacher. And I need your help."

"In what way could I possibly be of assistance?"

"If you three were close friends, then you *must* know where Jimmy Cox vanished. You're the only hope I have of saving him."

"I'm sure that it's too late for that."

Longarm's jaw muscles corded. "But what if you are wrong?! What if Jimmy *is* still alive and is being held hostage while someone tries to learn the whereabouts of that Spanish treasure in gold coins?!"

When the man didn't answer, Longarm said, "Preacher, are you really willing to take that chance? Or, put in another way, to take away what might be Jimmy's only chance to live?"

"No," the man whispered, "I'm not. What do you propose?"

"I propose that you lead me to Jimmy Cox. Or at least to the vicinity of where he told you he discovered those gold coins."

Preacher Dan pulled on his long white beard. "You seem very, very sure that I can do this."

"You're a man of faith," Longarm said. "I could hear faith in your words as you spoke over Eli's grave."

"I have faith that the Lord will judge those who have murdered my friends. I have no faith in you, Marshal. Or in any other man."

"Look," Longarm said, desperate to find the words that would win this deeply religious but stubborn man over to his side, "Eli didn't want to help me either, until I told him that there is a real possibility that Jimmy Cox is still alive, still being held captive until he either dies or breaks and tells where to find that treasure."

"How do you know this?"

"I know it," Longarm said, "because he sent me a newspaper and a note asking for help. That's why I came all the way to this Arizona Territory. And that's why I'm not going away until I either save Jimmy or give him a proper burial like Eli just received. But to do that, I *need* your help."

"Very well," Preacher Dan said after a long deliberation. "You shall have it to the extent that I can give it. But I warn you, I will not be a part or a party to vengeance. 'Vengeance is mine alone, sayeth the Lord.' "

"Yeah, I've heard that, but I've also heard 'An eye for an eye and a tooth for a tooth,' Preacher. But don't worry. I wouldn't think of asking you to take up arms against rapists and murderers. Or to save either of our lives if we are walking into our own graves."

"I don't fear death. Do you?"

"Yes," Longarm said, "I sure do. But then, I don't have your faith either."

"Perhaps it will grow as we go off into the desert."

"Perhaps."

The preacher frowned. "Do you have an outfit suitable for the desert country?"

"No, but I have the money to buy one."

"Just as good. Give me the money and I'll buy what you need for the journey we must take."

Longarm handed Preacher Dan the money.

"There," the man said, at last managing a smile. "You have just shown your first great act of faith in giving this money to a stranger."

"You aren't going to run out on me," Longarm replied. "And I'm not going to let you out of my sight."

The smile died. "Then you don't have any faith in me."

"I have faith in you," Longarm said, pivoting around and gazing back toward Wickenburg. "I also have a very strong belief that we are being watched right now by the man that cut Eli's throat last night. And *that's* why we're sticking close together until we leave this town."

The preacher's own eyes followed Longarm's back to town. He seemed lost in some deep inner dilemma, but he finally dipped his chin in assent and led the way to Wickenburg's largest general store, where they would outfit themselves for what Longarm was convinced would be a real ordeal.

Chapter 10

Longarm and the preacher named Dan rode out of Wickenburg headed southwest into the desert country.

"These are good horses," Longarm said as they rode along. "Better'n a man can usually expect when he rents out of a livery."

"I *own* the livery," Dan said, looking a little embarrassed. "Along with a few other local businesses."

Longarm was amazed. To look at Dan, you'd think he was a pauper. "You do?"

"That's right," the white-bearded man replied. "You act surprised, Marshal."

"I am," Longarm admitted.

"Is that because I dress very commonly and am called a preacher?"

"Partly. Preachers aren't known to have much in the way of money."

"Yes, but their true payment is everlasting life."

"I suppose."

They rode along in silence for a while, and then the preacher added, "Marshal, you're probably curious about how I come by money."

"That's none of my business."

"But it might be instructive," Dan argued, "so I'll tell you. About five years ago, the Lord drew me to a place far out in this desert and, just to test my faith, he put me in a terrible fix. Broke my leg, lost my horse and burro, had no water, and it was far hotter than it is right now."

"Sounds like you were in a real bad fix."

"Oh, I was!"

"So what happened?"

"When I began to die," Dan answered, "instead of getting angry at God, I told Him I was grateful to be leaving this earth and going to His side. I told Him that I'd been suffering from prospector's fever all my adult life and chasing earthly riches instead of eternal riches that His kingdom offered. I told Him that, if I ever had found gold, I probably would have just squandered it on sinful things—but that I was a changed man, thanks to my suffering. And then I said, 'Take me, God, 'cause I've suffered enough, and please do it quick!' "

"Obviously, He had other plans."

"Oh, yes, He did," Dan said. "Half crazed by thirst and blinded by the sun, I staggered into a deep hole."

"A hole?"

"Yep! It was a pit, really, filled with water from some deep underground spring. I tumbled into that water and it was like being baptized in the Jordan River. Suddenly, I could see again and my pain was gone. And at the bottom of that spring I found a sack full of gold nuggets."

84

"That's amazing."

"Not quite as amazing as you might think. Why, less than fifty miles south it is not so uncommon to find water trickling sweetly out of sun-blasted canyon walls. And as for the gold, it was God's miracle."

"What did you do with the gold?"

"I prayed long and hard over that," Dan replied. "At first, I thought that I should give it all away to those less fortunate than myself. But that wasn't what the Lord wanted."

"How did you know?"

"Every time I gave it to some poor soul, he'd just use it to commit a mighty sin and then generally wind up filling the pockets of bad men and soiled women."

"Yeah," Longarm said, "I can believe that. So what *did* you do?"

"I invested it in businesses. I figured that I'd donate half to myself and half to God's works."

"To charity."

"That's right. And you see, our missing friend, Jimmy Cox, became one of my favorite charities. Oh, I grubstaked others, but Jimmy and poor Eli were by far my favorites. They were both rough as the rest . . . and profane, but they had Christian hearts and would help anyone in their need. And I've seen them do it many a time. So, I helped them."

"Did Jimmy ever tell you where he found those gold Spanish coins?"

"He wanted to tell me, but I wouldn't let him."

"Why?"

Dan scratched his long white beard. "Well, to begin with, I didn't believe he'd really found those coins."

"You sound like you changed your mind."

"I did! Jimmy had too many of them, and it was clear

that they were the real thing. At first, some folks in Wickenburg thought they were Mexican brass, but they quickly changed their minds. I'll tell you, it caused quite a stir."

"Any chance that the outlaw Hank Bass had something to do with Jimmy's disappearance?" Longarm asked.

"Of course there is. Bass is a very evil man and those that ride for him are no better."

"Well, Preacher, they don't ride for him anymore."

Dan cocked a bushy eyebrow, but he didn't ask exactly what Longarm meant by that statement. "We'll be riding today and most of tomorrow to get to where I think Jimmy disappeared."

"I assume that will be the same place that he found the Spanish coins."

"That's right. We'll camp there and have a look around. I went there right after Jimmy disappeared but couldn't find anything to tell me what happened to him. But then, I'm not good at that sort of thing and you have the professional eye. I'm hoping there are a few clues, although the wind blows pretty hard out here and everything might have been brushed away."

"You think he's dead, don't you?"

Dan sadly nodded his head. "Yes, I'm afraid that I do. I'm very afraid that whoever slit poor Eli's throat also killed Jimmy. It seems to me that the two events must be related."

"I agree," Longarm said. "And it seems to me that whoever is behind all this must believe that there is still a lot of Spanish gold out here yet to be found."

"Why do you say that?"

"Because," Longarm replied, "what other reason

would they have for killing Eli after I talked to him about Jimmy?''

"To keep from being identified?''

"No," Longarm said, "I didn't know Eli at all, but you did and I'm sure you agree that the man would have identified Jimmy's killers if he'd known their identities.''

"You're right," Dan said, nodding his head. "See, you have the mind for this sort of thing. I don't.''

"Did Jimmy have any relatives?" Longarm asked.

"No. He never married. Always been a loner. I think that Eli, myself, and you must have been the only ones that he really trusted. You see, if a man stays out here in this desert by himself for too long, he starts to talk out loud, at first to his burro, if he has one, then to himself.''

"Is that a fact?''

"It is," Dan insisted. "I have carried on daylong conversations with myself and my burro. The three of us have argued and even almost come to blows a time or two. Now, I *also* talk to the Lord a lot, but someone like Eli or Jimmy, they don't, and so they get to hearing strange voices.''

"You mean, in their heads?''

"That's right," Dan replied. "Sometimes the voices are friendly, but sometimes not. And after a long while, prospectors just sort of go a little crazy. I'm sure you've seen them wandering around frontier mining towns, muttering things to themselves. Arguing back and forth. It's pretty common.''

"I doubt that Jimmy was crazy," Longarm said. "He'd been a prospector a long, long time when I met him and he wasn't crazy.''

"He changed some after he found those Spanish coins

87

and started our big Wickenburg gold rush. People were always trying to get him drunk so he'd tell them where he found those coins. And they followed him everywhere. Jimmy got to where he wouldn't hardly come into Wickenburg anymore.''

"I see." Longarm squinted into the heat waves and watched a dust devil dance across the desert floor. This was, he knew, bad country to get into without a guide who knew the watering holes.

They rode all that day and made a dry camp at sundown. Dan had bought some big skin bags and filled them with water, but their two thirsty horses could have drunk it all and lots more. There was also fifty pounds of oats tied to the back of each saddle, so the horses had plenty to eat.

"If we get an early start," Dan said, "we'll arrive at that deep spring by mid-morning."

"The one where you found gold?"

"That's right. From there, we go on a few miles farther and then I'll show you about where I think that Jimmy discovered those Spanish coins. Would have been a lot better off never to have found them, don't you agree?"

"Yes," Longarm said, "I do."

That evening, they ate well because the preacher had paid someone to pack them a fine supper with beef, potatoes, and even a couple of thick slabs of apple pie. Longarm and Dan talked only a short while and then they collapsed on their blankets and went right to sleep.

When Longarm awoke the next morning, Dan was frying salt pork and making biscuits. He had even brewed a pot of coffee and looked happy and content. Dan gave Longarm a warm smile of greeting. "Mornin', Marshal Long!"

"Custis. And yes, it is a fine morning."

And indeed it was. The sun was floating off the horizon, and its soft crimson glow made the Arizona desert look almost hospitable at this hour. Sunrise and sunset were the finest hours in country like this, and Longarm accepted a cup of coffee from Dan and sat cross-legged on his blankets to enjoy it.

"You know, Marshal, most people think that the desert is a hard, awful place, but it isn't. Want to hear my theory on deserts?"

"Sure."

"They are meant to be experienced at night."

"In the dark?"

"It never really gets all that dark on the desert. You have starlight and moonlight and the sage get silvery so that it all shines. You must know that the critters that live out here sleep in the daytime and only come out at night."

"Yeah, I've heard that."

"It's true! The desert comes alive with goings-on at night and it just kind of buttons up in the daytime—even in winter when it can get cold."

Longarm finished his coffee, ate a good breakfast, and then enjoyed another cup of coffee before they packed up their things and continued on to the southwest. The day was growing quite warm when Dan finally drew in on his reins and pointed to a cluster of rocks out of which spurted some mesquite.

"Over there is where the spring is and where the Lord led me to that gold."

Longarm nodded. "Can you point out where you think Jimmy found those Spanish coins?"

"Sure," Dan said, raising a finger. "You see that

notch in the blue ridge straight on past the rocks about ten miles?''

"Yes."

"Well, there are some caves dug out of the sandstone cliffs up there. I expect that is where Jimmy found that Spanish treasure.''

"What gives you that idea?''

"He told me," Dan said. "Pointed them out to me once, saying that he had found some old Spanish armor. You know, rusted helmets and breastplates. And not far away, he discovered the skeletons of their owners in some of those caves. I expect that we will find them too.''

Longarm could feel his pulse quicken. "Why, I don't see why not." He squinted and then urged his horse into a trot.

"Hey!" Dan shouted. "Go easy on my horse out here! This is hard country. Bow a tendon or give him a rock bruise or a cactus spine in the hock and you're on foot, Marshal!''

Longarm knew that Dan was speaking the truth. But he hadn't exactly put steel to the flanks of his animal and he was getting awfully anxious to unravel the mystery of Jimmy's disappearance.

It seemed to take forever for them to reach the hidden spring where Dan had found his salvation. They watered their horses and filled their canteens.

"Told you this water was sweet, didn't I?" Dan said, smacking his lips.

"You did and you weren't exaggerating one bit," Longarm said. "I can't even imagine how happy you must have been if you were out here staggering around and ready to die of thirst.''

"I think the Lord put this spring here just to save me

and open my eyes to see that we are here to serve our fellow man, not oppress or kill him.''

"Sometimes, Preacher, our 'fellow man' needs to be killed,'' Longarm argued. "Hank Bass is a prime example, as is whoever cut poor Eli's throat.''

Dan shook his head, but Longarm could not tell if he was in disagreement or just generally depressed by the grim subject. Either way, Longarm didn't really care. When he found the men who had killed old Jimmy and Eli, then justice would be swift and final. Maybe that was entirely the wrong attitude for a man who carried a badge, but Longarm couldn't help feeling that way.

"All right,'' Dan said after they had rested and replenished their water supplies. "Let's go find those Spanish conquistador caves and skeletons.''

"Let's just hope we don't find Jimmy's skeleton with them,'' Longarm said.

Dan nodded, then he went against his own advice as he forced his mount into a trot despite the unforgiving and intensifying heat of the desert sun.

Chapter 11

Longarm threw up his right hand as a signal for Preacher Dan to rein in his horse, then he dismounted and made sure that his shotgun was loaded and ready to fire in case someone was watching them from the rocks. He handed his reins to the older man and removed his hat, then started forward.

"I don't think we have much to worry about," Dan whispered. "It's not likely that anyone is here."

"Why take the chance?"

"But even if there were someone here, Marshal Long, I'd sure hope that you would try not to kill them."

"What?"

"You're a federal lawman—not an executioner."

Longarm spun around on his boot heel. "That's right, I *am* a federal marshal, but that doesn't mean I'm also a fool! And if the same murdering son of a bitch that cut Eli's throat and probably did the same thing to

Jimmy is waiting up there for me, you can bet your life that I'm going to shoot to kill!''

''With a shotgun that big, you could hardly do otherwise.''

''That's right. So just stay back here with the horses while I go up and scout around. It'll be better for the both of us that way.''

''Very well,'' Dan said. ''Be careful.''

''Count on it.''

Off in the distance, Longarm could see a trail leading up into the rocks and it was clear that it had been used within the last few months. But he could not tell if it had been used in just the last few days.

There was an open place that he had to cross without any cover whatsoever. Longarm judged it to be perhaps twenty-five yards long and well exposed to the higher rocks. If there was an ambusher or two up above, this was where they would try to make their kill.

Longarm hunkered down behind some brush and sleeved sweat from his brow. He would wait awhile even though there was no indication that this place was inhabited. Besides, in a very short while, the sun would be burning directly over his left shoulder and into the rocks. It would create problems if there was an ambusher in waiting.

Longarm flicked a couple of big black ants off the back of his hand. He looked around to make sure that he wasn't in the company of a rattlesnake or a scorpion, then he stretched out to full length and relaxed. He would have been quite happy to take a catnap, except that the sun was too bright and hot and the damned ants were a constant bother.

Time passed pleasantly enough, and every few minutes Longarm would tilt his hat back from his face and gaze up at the rocks and those sandstone caverns. He couldn't see inside them because he was too low and they were a good fifty feet higher in elevation. And as for some dying Spanish conquistadors ending up in a hell like this, hundreds of miles from the nearest reliable river, well, Longarm could not imagine the anguish they must have felt or even why they would come so far to get themselves into such a terrible situation. But that was another time and another issue that he had no business wasting his time thinking about right now.

When the sun was blazing into the face of the rocks and the higher sandstone caverns, Longarm decided that he might as well make his move. Yes, it would have been better to have circled around behind for a safer approach, but he knew that Dan would have complained about the extra work for his horses. It would also have been better to make this move at night, but Longarm felt time was too precious. Besides, he was so anxious about finding something, *anything* related to Jimmy's disappearance that he was determined not to wait any longer.

Longarm gathered the shotgun in his hands, took a couple of deep breaths, and then rushed forward, eyes riveted on the nearest rocks. No sooner had he jumped forward than a rifle shot boomed from above, and Longarm felt a searing fire across his leg and went tumbling. The shotgun spilled from his grasp and a second rifle bullet ricocheted off the rock beside his face, momentarily blinding Longarm. Knowing it was unlikely that the ambusher would miss again if he didn't start moving, Longarm rolled sideways as fast as he could until he dropped into a shallow crevasse in the rocks. Still fighting to clear his vision, Longarm dragged out his six-gun and fired blindly upward in the general direction of the ambusher. His bullet was more than matched by the return fire.

"Damn!" Longarm swore, angry at himself for getting into such a bad fix. No one had to tell him that the rifleman above had all the advantages. As if to reinforce the fact, the ambusher resumed firing. He couldn't quite reach Longarm with a bullet, but it was very close and he might get a ricochet and get lucky.

"Preacher Dan!" Longarm cried, his voice echoing through the boulders. "I need your help!"

There was no answer except for the retort of more rifle bullets.

"Dan, get the rifle and give me some covering fire!" Longarm pleaded, not really expecting that the preacher would do anything more than rattle the ambusher and perhaps give Longarm a chance to escape back down the slope to good cover.

Maybe an hour passed, but it felt more like a day as Longarm recovered his vision and waited for either Dan to come to his aid or the sun to go down so that he could slither off without getting drilled with a rifle slug. Then, suddenly, Longarm heard brush cracking downslope. He twisted around to see Preacher Dan standing with the rifle held loosely in his hands. The fool was just gawking up at the rocks.

"Get down!" Longarm shouted.

His warning was too late. The ambusher shot Dan in the shoulder, spinning him completely around. The only thing that saved Dan's life was that he fell over backward into brush before the next rifle slug could ventilate his empty head.

Longarm was furious! With the ambusher's attention momentarily diverted, he hobbled forward, scooping up his shotgun. Three long but limping strides carried him up the slope to cover. When the ambusher realized his mistake and stood up to try to get a better line of fire, Longarm opened up with both barrels of his shotgun.

The range was probably too far, but the shotgun's shells packed rare force and Longarm actually saw the ambusher lift completely off his feet and then fly backward as if he had been jerked over by an invisible chain. He also saw the mushrooming crimson smear that had been the ambusher's upper body. No question about it, the son of a bitch was dead.

Longarm glanced down at the crease in his pants. He was bleeding pretty good but knew that he'd suffered no permanent damage. Nothing that a few stitches or even a good bandage job wouldn't fix. But Preacher Dan was another matter, and Longarm was almost certain that the old man had taken a fatal bullet in the shoulder.

"Dammit, Dan!" he swore, hobbling as fast as he could over to his friend's side and dragging him out of the bushes so that he could be examined. "What were you thinking when you jumped up there and gave that man a clear target?!"

"I was thinking that, if the Lord was calling, I was ready to go."

Longarm snorted. What could you do with such a man as this? Dan really didn't care if he lived or died.

"Well," Longarm said, "the Lord *wasn't* calling because you are still alive."

"Maybe I'll get gangrene," Dan said almost hopefully.

Longarm tore open Dan's shirt and studied the wound. It was nasty, but the blood wasn't real bright red as it would have been if Dan had taken a slug through the lung. "Maybe you'll make it after all," he said. "Roll over and let me see if the slug passed on through."

"And if it didn't?"

"Then," Longarm said, "I'll have no choice but to cut it out and that can be pretty rough."

"I can take it," Dan gritted.

"I'm sure that you can."

"Did you kill that fella up above?"

"Blew his murdering head right off his shoulders," Longarm said with a tight grin. "He won't be ambushing anyone else—or cutting their throats."

"Maybe he isn't the one," Dan said, looking pale as Longarm eased him over so that he could see that the bullet had not passed completely through the shoulder.

"I'm going to have to dig this bullet out or you're a goner," Longarm said. "Either that, or try to get you back to Wickenburg before you get blood poisoning."

"The doc in Wickenburg is just a tooth puller. You go ahead and do your best. If I die, ain't no big matter."

"It is to me," Longarm said. "I brought you out here, I feel responsible. Besides, you pretty well saved my life."

Dan had been lying still, breathing hard with his eyes closed. But at Longarm's words, he managed a smile. "I did?"

"That's right."

"Well, then, I don't feel so bad about that other fella dying. I mean, I guess he deserved it."

"Yes, he sure did. Now hold still and grit your teeth while I dig this slug out of your back. I think I can see it just under the skin. It almost went through."

Longarm cut Dan's flesh just under the shoulder blade. The blood really started to flow, but that wasn't necessarily bad because it would carry out the infection. Dan didn't do much other than grunt like a rutting boar while Longarm fished out the rifle slug, then rinsed the wound with his canteen and finally bandaged it tightly.

"Am I going to make it?"

"Of course you are," Longarm said, taking care of his own leg wound. "But I have to tell you that we are both going to be a little under the weather for a few days."

"Give us time to rest up and explore these caves," Dan whispered between clenched teeth. "Maybe find poor Jimmy's grave."

"I doubt that they'd have bothered to even bury Jimmy," Longarm said. "These kind of men aren't generally so kindly disposed, if you know what I mean."

"I guess that I do," Dan said.

"Let's go on up to the caves," Longarm suggested. "I'll bet that there is food and water waiting up there. We can rest up tonight, then tomorrow start poking around."

"What about our horses?"

"All right," Longarm said, "I'll lead them up after the sun goes down. We've got grain, water, and hobbles. There's enough feed up here to keep them going awhile."

"Okay," Dan agreed, allowing Longarm to help him to his feet. Dan leaned heavily on him as they slowly made their way up to the caves.

Despite the fact that they were both bleeding and in considerable pain, Longarm made a slight detour so that the preacher did not have to witness the terrible sight of the headless ambusher. If Dan realized that fact, he didn't say anything. They both collapsed in the first cave they reached, gasping for breath.

"You wait here," Longarm said. "I'll be back soon."

"You going for my horses?"

"Not until I've had a little look around," Longarm said.

"Don't make it too long," Dan fretted. "Those horses might just have broke away during all that shooting. If they did, we're in a terrible fix 'cause they'll head straight back to Wickenburg."

Longarm realized with a jolt that Dan was right. Forgetting about the caves, he hurried back down the slope and made his way through the brush to where they'd left the horses.

"Well, gawdammit!" he swore, seeing a faint trail of dust leading off toward Wickenburg. "Dammit anyway!"

The only good part was that Dan, always worrying about the condition of his horses, had unsaddled them during the long afternoon wait, so at least their supplies, the Winchester rifle, and Longarm's other belongings had not gone south with the runaways.

Still, as Longarm gazed out at the merciless desert, he could not help but feel a powerful sense of foreboding. Things could have been worse, but they could also have been a hell of a lot better.

Chapter 12

Longarm wasn't in a very good mood as he hobbled back up to the caves with his rifle, their water, and a few of their supplies. His leg wound was throbbing like the devil, and the preacher looked very pale and feverish where he lay stretched out in the cave.

"The horses ran away," he told his suffering friend. "We're stuck out here, and neither one of us is in any shape to hike back to Wickenburg for help."

"We've got food and you can hunt rabbits," Dan said. "And maybe we'll find other things to eat here."

"I expect that we will," Longarm agreed. "And that spring where you found your gold isn't but a long day's walk, so I'm not worried about dying, if that's what you mean."

"Have you looked around yet?"

"No," Longarm said, collapsing on the floor of the small cave and tightening the bandage on his leg because he was bleeding again. "But I'm about played out for the moment and it's getting damned hot outside. Think I'll just rest this leg and my eyes for a while."

"You do that," Dan said, nodding with approval. "I've spent most of my life in this desert country and the best thing to do is take a long siesta in the afternoon. Get your business done early in the evening and late in the day when it's cooler. The Mexican people are smart enough to understand that simple fact of life."

Longarm laid his head on his saddlebags, knowing that he would go right to sleep and expecting that old Dan would do the same. The preacher was in rough shape and had lost a great deal of blood from his shoulder wound. The man's eyes were sunken in his face and his complexion was the color of wax. Longarm knew that Dan was trying to put on a good show, but he was weak and suffering. It would take weeks for Dan to regain his strength, but they didn't have that much time. A way would have to be found to get the preacher back to Wickenburg where he could receive proper rest and medical attention. But right now, damned if Longarm could think of one.

They both slept right through the day and that night, waking up at dawn the next morning. As the light grew stronger, Longarm got up, stretched, and then hobbled back down to where the horses had escaped. He collected the rest of their supplies and lugged everything up to the cave. His leg was very stiff and painful, but the bleeding had stopped and, when Longarm rebandaged the wound, he was happy to see that it was healing without infection. Once again, he'd been real lucky.

After breakfast, Longarm went over to the headless

101

corpse and dragged it over to a little rock slide. It was truly a ghastly sight, and even a seasoned lawman like Custis almost gagged as he searched the man's empty pockets looking for some clue as to his identity. Finding none, he removed the man's side arm. It took very little time and effort to climb a few yards up a nearby rock slide and get enough shale moving to bury the hideous corpse. When that was done, Longarm felt much better and took a moment to glance up at a circling buzzard.

"Not this time," he said to the ugly scavenger as he hobbled off to inspect the caves. He was anxious to see what kind of supplies he'd find and if there was any trace of Jimmy Cox that would give him a clue as to the old prospector's fate.

There was a series of caves, all of them cut out of the sandstone by the action of spring runoffs. Each varied in size, but only a few were large enough so that a body of men could enter them and take shelter. In the first one of size, Longarm discovered the supplies. It was clear that this was where the ambusher had been living, and it took only a few minutes to see that there was a good supply of food, although mostly just coffee, flour, and dried beans. There were, however, casks of precious water, enough to keep him and Dan going for several weeks.

Longarm also saw evidence that several other men had recently been living in this large sandstone cave. A pile of tin cans and other assorted trash including many empty whiskey bottles told him plenty. He found prospecting tools too. Picks, shovels, and even a few sticks of dynamite.

"They haven't found what they were looking for yet," he muttered to himself as he went back outside and began to explore the rest of the caves.

It took only a few minutes to glance inside some of the smaller caves, but in one he was half turned and leaving when he froze, then slowly revolved back around and stared. Inside, he found a skeleton and it was wearing a rusty breastplate. Longarm dropped down on his hands and knees and eased inside, wondering if there were more skeletons. He quickly realized that this particular cave, though small in circumference, was at least twenty feet deep. As he eased past the skeleton, he saw more scattered bones including four skulls which had been placed by someone so that they rested in a neat little circle, face to noseless face.

Longarm lit a match and held it in front of him. He discovered several more pieces of rusty armor in such a deteriorated condition that it was impossible to guess their original purpose. The cave was very cool and dark, and Longarm was sure that the dying Spaniards had probably taken their last refuge here as if crawling into their own crypts. Unfortunately, their decaying bodies would have drawn scavengers who devoured them and then scattered their bones. Someone, perhaps the man Longarm had killed or one of his friends, had taken sick humor in putting the skulls in that little circle as if they had been talking at each other for the last few centuries.

Longarm backed out of the cave and went to finish his explorations. In the next to the last cave, he found signs that a good deal of excavation had taken place. The cave was more like a funnel, some six or seven feet round, and its natural shape narrowed like the point of a cone. Longarm found candles and holders and lit one. He crept back into the cave and saw that the original back wall, which could not have been more than a yard square, had been opened up just enough to reveal another cavern. To enter it, Longarm had to get down on his knees, turn sideways, and squeeze through. Back here, the air was cool and still. Longarm shoved his candle out before him and beheld a very large cavern, one big enough to have housed at least a dozen men and maybe a few horses, if they had been able to reach it.

Longarm stood up in this larger, deeper cavern and gazed all around. It was clear that this had been the place where the Spaniards must have opened up and then lived in until they became extremely weak or had died. There were bones all over the floor, and someone had smashed the skulls beyond recognition. Longarm found dozens of shattered whiskey bottles here too. Dark black smoke smudges told him that hundreds of campfires had burned in this cavern. He studied the walls, hoping to see some early Indian petroglyphs, but there were none.

Longarm felt very sure that Jimmy Cox or some earlier prospector had discovered this secret cavern and used it for extended periods. As in the smaller cave where he'd found the circle of skulls, this one also had a large pile of trash. Longarm moved over to sift through it and that was when he found an old burlap sack stenciled with the letters, *JC*.

"Oh, Jimmy," he said with a deep sigh of sadness, "I don't give you much in the way of odds as for being alive. I'll bet anything that I find your bones somewhere around close. Or maybe your killers took the time and trouble to cover you up just like I did to the ambusher."

Longarm spent a quarter of an hour in the cave. By then, he was convinced that he could find nothing else that would give him any useful information about Jimmy Cox. So he retreated from the cave as his candle flickered low and went back to tell Dan about his findings.

When he was finished, Dan said, "It does sound

pretty grim. But, Marshal, we can't just give up on Jimmy. He could still be alive.''

"No," Longarm said. "They followed and then obviously murdered him somewhere around here. I just wish I hadn't used my shotgun on the one that was left behind. If he were still alive, we'd have all our answers to this riddle. We'd know the real story about what happened to Jimmy.''

"What do you think the chances are of others returning?''

Longarm eased his wounded leg out before him and sat down heavily. He felt a little unsteady and realized that he was going to have to go slower for the next couple of days, if he was to get strong again.

"I think that whoever did this hasn't found what they wanted. Or maybe they did find all the Spanish treasure but, for some reason, believe that there is still more. Jimmy might have played that card, hoping to keep himself alive.''

"It makes sense, doesn't it?'' Dan said.

"Yes. Let's suppose that *you* were Jimmy Cox.''

"I'd rather not," Dan said. "He was a godless man.''

"Never mind the moral judgments for now, Preacher. Just suppose that you were Jimmy and had found the Spanish coins here. You had used some of them to pay off your doctor and other medical bills, then had come back out to collect the rest of the treasure but had been followed.''

"I wouldn't have allowed myself to be followed," Dan said. "I mean, wouldn't he have *expected* something like that to happen, given the greed of most men?''

"Sure," Longarm said. "And if he had been followed by just one or two killers, he probably would have been able to shake them and reach this place without anyone knowing it. However, if there were a good number of killers . . .''

"You mean a gang of outlaws.''

"That's right, Dan. I mean a gang like Hank Bass used to have.''

"I see.''

"It fits,'' Longarm said. "Bass is the most likely candidate for this job. He'd have had enough men to scatter them across this part of the desert so that one or two of them would have seen Jimmy coming. And Jimmy would have been looking *back* not forward. Anyway, I think that is what happened. They watched Jimmy come straight to these caves. After that, they would have caught and probably tied him up, then sent for the rest of the Bass gang.''

"And then they would have tried to force Jimmy to tell them where he'd found the Spanish coins.''

"Exactly,'' Longarm said. "And we both know how mule stubborn Jimmy was. He'd have fought to the last breath and held his secret to the end.''

"But what if . . .''

"If what?'' Longarm asked.

"What if there was no more Spanish treasure?''

"That's possible,'' Longarm said. "But put yourself in Jimmy's shoes. If there was no treasure left to be found, why would you risk your life to return, knowing that everyone in this part of Arizona would be trying to follow you?''

"Good point,'' Dan admitted. "So you *do* think that there is still some treasure.''

"Yes. But what I think doesn't mean anything at all. It's what Jimmy thought that was important and what he managed to convince his captors.''

"And he'd want to convince them that he *knew* the

location of more treasure. That would be his only hope.''

"Sure," Longarm agreed. "It was his only card to play. He'd have had to keep silent, yet give his captors hints that he knew something.''

"But how long could he play that sort of game?"

"Not long, I'm afraid. Bass and his gang—or maybe some other bunch—would have tired of the game very quickly. And they wouldn't have been sitting still waiting either. No sir. They'd have been tearing these caves up. Scattering conquistador bones and poking and picking into every crevasse, hoping to find more gold coins.''

"But they didn't."

Longarm shrugged. "Who knows. If they did find a few more coins, it would have fueled their already mountainous greed. If they didn't find any coins, that too would have been fuel to their fire and increased their frustration and anger until . . ."

"Until they killed poor Jimmy."

"That's right," Longarm grimly replied. "The kind of men that would cut Eli's throat would not have been long on patience. I'll bet that Jimmy didn't last a week and that whatever time he last had here was hell on earth.''

"God forgive them," Preacher Dan breathed.

"Well," Longarm said, "I think I've killed them all except Hank Bass. And, unless I'm badly mistaken, he'll be coming back here.''

"Alone?"

"Maybe, maybe not. He might recruit a few other cutthroats. I expect that he will.''

"And how will we stand up against them?"

"I don't know that answer either," Longarm replied. "But the good news is that this time *we'll* be the ones up here on the high ground and ready to spring the surprise."

Longarm laced his fingers behind his head. "But I got to know something, Preacher."

"Yes?"

"Am I going to be doing this all alone, or can I count on your help?"

"I don't want to kill anyone. I don't believe that I have the right to take a human life."

"What about in the name of self-defense?"

"I'll give it some thought."

"You had better come up with the right answers," Longarm said, unable to hide his growing exasperation. "Because, if Hank Bass does bring friends, I'm going to need your help."

"I would be more than willing to help you capture them alive."

"Not much chance of that, I'm afraid. Because when they come—and they *will* come—it will be a fight to the death. We don't have horses, remember? Your damned horses broke free and ran away. So we've got to take *their* horses in order to get the hell back to Wickenburg."

"We could walk."

"Not a chance. I got a bad leg and you got a bad shoulder. So we'll wait for whoever killed Jimmy Cox to return and then we'll take their horses. They're not going to want us to do that, Preacher. And they're going to try and stop us with bullets. Do you understand what I'm saying?"

"Of course I do. You're saying that we have to kill in order not to be killed."

"That's right," Longarm said. "Now, can you shoot straight or have you always been a damned pacifist?"

Dan flushed with anger. "I'll have you know that I've been in some pretty rough fights during my younger days. In fact, I shot . . ."

The words trailed off like smoke in the desert wind. "What have you shot, Preacher?"

Dan turned away, and when he spoke, his voice was low and strained. "I've shot men too. Killed them."

"Good!" Longarm pronounced. "Then you're up to the task and that's what I'll expect when it comes time to do what must be done."

Dan muttered something in reply, but Longarm couldn't and really didn't want to hear what else the wounded man had to say.

"I'm ready for another nap," he said, glancing out at the sun. "Getting hot again."

When Dan still didn't bother to reply, Longarm stretched out in the cool dust of the cave floor and went right to sleep.

Chapter 13

In the slow, hot days that followed, Longarm spent most of his time inside the sandstone caves looking for clues and coins. He found several of the latter and some interesting Spanish relics like buttons and buckles. But most of all, he was looking for Jimmy's body, and it wasn't until the fourth day that he finally found it. The outlaws hadn't been as clever as Longarm with his instant rock-slide grave. They'd actually taken the time to bury poor old Jimmy, and although the corpse was very old and decayed, there was enough left to identify the prospector.

Longarm took the discovery hard. Jimmy had once saved his life, and the old goat had been a true friend. Longarm used his knife to whittle a nice wooden cross made out of a wooden box, then he carved Jimmy's name in it while Preacher Dan said a few words of prayerful farewell.

When their little service was over, Longarm walked out into the desert until the moon came over the horizon and he tried to get a grip on his feelings. *He lived a very long, full life*, Longarm told himself. *Jimmy Cox was one of the very rare people I've ever met who did exactly what he wanted to do when he wanted to do it. I'm sure that, if he had a second chance at life, he'd play it out exactly the same way, even knowing his sad end.*

Longarm felt better when he returned to their camp. He slept well that night and continued to wait and recover. His leg was healing and Dan's shoulder was also coming along just fine. But where was Hank Bass and his boys? Surely they'd be back, wouldn't they?

It took another four days before Longarm spotted the horsemen coming across the desert. There were five, and he watched them for a long time to see if they might rein off and go in another direction. But they did not.

"Dan, I'm going to give you the shotgun this time and I'll handle the Winchester. Even you can't miss with that big scattergun."

"I'm still not sure that I can do this."

"Well, then," Longarm said, "we'll probably be killed. And while I know that doesn't mean a whole hell of a lot to you, it does to me. Besides, these will be the same ones that murdered poor Jimmy."

"Yeah," Dan said, "I expect that's true."

Longarm loaded and checked the double-barreled shotgun, then handed it to Dan. "I'm sorry I have to ask for your help, but the odds are too great against me alone. I can probably kill one, maybe even two, before they reach cover, but that would still leave three."

"Yeah," Dan said, handling the shotgun. "All right, I'll do my part."

"Thanks," Longarm said with relief. "That's all I

111

wanted to know. Now, you move into that cave and stay hidden until they get right up here."

"We're going to let them do that?"

"Yes," Longarm said. "Despite what you might think, I'll order them to surrender and drop their weapons. If they don't, then it's going to be war and I expect you to fire my biggest cannon. Trouble is, we need to take at least one of them alive. I mean to find out exactly who killed Jimmy."

"Okay," Dan said in reluctant agreement as he started for the cave.

"And, Dan?"

"Yeah?"

"You won't miss if you pull the triggers and have that shotgun pointed in the right direction."

Dan nodded without a word and then disappeared in the cave to wait. Longarm inspected his Winchester and six-gun. When he was completely satisfied that they were in good working order, he hunkered down behind some high rocks and watched the approaching riders. They were a bad-looking bunch. Two were Indians and rode bareback with rifles resting across the bare withers of their skinny ponies. The other three were white men of the roughest kind. One was a bearded giant and the other two were thin, hard-looking men that Longarm judged to be professional killers. Longarm decided to shoot this pair first, then try for the two Indians. He'd save the giant for last because the man was the largest target and might be a shade slower than his leaner companions.

Because of the steepness of the slope, the outlaws were forced to dismount and tie their horses several hundred feet downhill, which was very much to Longarm's liking as he fixed the first of the gunfighters in his rifle

112

sights. It was crazy to give them a warning, but he was no executioner and he had promised Dan that he would at least offer them a chance to surrender.

"I'm a U.S. marshal!" he shouted. "Throw down your weapons and . . ."

Every last one of the outlaws went for their weapons without any thought of surrender. Longarm shot one of the gunfighters in the chest and managed to drop the other one before he could return fire. The Indians were his third and fourth targets, but they were too quick and clever to stand and stare into the low sun trying to identify a target. Instead, they dove into some brush before Longarm could unleash a third bullet.

The giant *was* slow of mind and body. He chose to attack on foot, and Longarm would have killed him easily enough except that the fool lost his footing and crashed into the brush. At that very instant, Dan chose to fire the shotgun and a blast swept harmlessly over the giant's head. But the fool jumped up, and Dan fired a second blast that nearly beheaded the giant. It was a terrible, grisly thing to see that huge body crash to earth and then begin to flop around in the grip of death.

Longarm had to turn away for a moment as the sounds of their gunfire echoed off into the hills and then everything became very silent. He glanced over his shoulder and saw Dan holding the smoking shotgun with a horrified expression marking his haggard old face.

"Dan, get down!" Longarm shouted.

Longarm's warning came too late. One of the Indians popped up like a cork in a tub and shot Dan, who staggered back into the cave.

"Dan!" Longarm shouted.

There was no answer and Longarm felt a sudden rage, but he'd been in too many fights to do anything foolish or rash. He'd only seen Dan for an instant and didn't know if the man was dead or alive, but it seemed pretty obvious that he wasn't going to be much help.

Longarm caught a glimpse of one of the Indians moving toward the horses. Suddenly, he knew that he had to stampede their animals so that the Indians could not either get to their canteens or escape and perhaps find some willing friends.

Stampeding the horses was easy and only took a few well-placed bullets to send the five animals rearing back on their reins and breaking free. Longarm saw an Indian leap up and try to catch one of the ponies. He snapped off a rifle shot and the Indian disappeared into the brush.

"Did I get him?" he asked himself out loud.

Longarm didn't think so. Or, if he had, he figured that the Indian was only grazed because he had dived rather than fallen into the brush. Longarm glanced up at the sky. It was almost sundown, and he knew that the Indians were probably Apache and that they would wait until after dark to make their move. The trouble was, would they come after him, or simply leave and go after their stampeded horses? Longarm figured they'd do the latter. Apache were brave, but they were also very smart, meaning that they might decide to leave, get help, and return when *they* had the advantage of surprise.

I can't allow that to happen, Longarm thought. *I've got to go out there and finish them off or they'll come back with reinforcements and I'm as good as dead without a horse to ride away on.*

Longarm cursed his decision to shoot the two gunfighters first. He would have been better off to kill these Indians. A couple of gunfighters would have acted very predictably and come after him, making things much, much easier.

114

Darkness fell gently across the desert and the sky flamed with rose colors. The air cooled and the heat-constricted earth seemed to sigh with relief as the first stars faintly appeared in the indigo sky.

Longarm began to retreat until his back was to the cave. He ducked inside to find Preacher Dan still breathing but unconscious. Working quickly in the darkness, Longarm groped for the man's bullet wound. When he found it, he knew that he had to get Dan to a doctor or the man was finished. He was probably finished anyway, but perhaps not. The fresh bullet would had struck the old prospector in the ribs and mostly likely had broken several, but Longarm was able to determine that the Apache bullet had passed through Dan's body on a trajectory that might not have ripped apart any vital organs. The wound was still bleeding, so Longarm did the best bandaging job that he could, given his difficult circumstances.

So, Longarm thought, as he assessed his predicament and the necessity of having to go after two Apache in the brush, *things aren't looking too damned good.*

He checked his weapons and started to leave the cave, his mind already focused on the problems he was about to tackle. But some inner warning caused him to step sideways and that was what saved his life. One of the Apache had gotten above the mouth of the cave and had jumped at Longarm's back with a drawn knife. But even though he had missed burying his knife in Longarm, he was agile enough to land on his feet and attack with a murderous scream.

Longarm didn't have time to draw his pistol. In fact, it was all that he could do to raise his forearm and block the downward thrust of the Apache's knife. He slammed the Indian in the groin with his knee and heard the man grunt with pain, then reel backward but attack again. This time Longarm had a moment and he used it to go for his six-gun. But the Indian came too fast and, before Longarm could make his cross draw, the Apache knife was slicing at his arm, opening it wide and causing the blood to flow and the gun to fall to the ground.

"All right," Longarm said, knowing he could not regain the weapon. "Let's finish this."

The Apache was more than ready and began to circle, knife blade held upward, legs and back bent. Longarm was damned worried. In the first place, the Apache was smaller but probably quicker, and that was all to his advantage. In the second place, the second Apache was probably very close and about to join the fight. Longarm knew that with his gun spilled somewhere in the darkness he stood no chance whatsoever against two determined Apache.

"Come on!" he hissed, teeth drawn back and blood flowing warmly down his left arm.

His enemy lunged forward, and Longarm tried to grab his wrist but failed. Again, he felt the Apache's blade rip across his flesh as hot and burning as a cattleman's branding iron. Longarm reached for the derringer that he carried at the end of his watch chain. The Apache saw the movement, but he didn't react quickly enough, so Longarm drew out the derringer and shot him dead in his tracks.

Not worrying about the Apache, Longarm jumped forward, hands sweeping blindly across the ground in search of his spilled six-gun. It seemed to take forever to locate the weapon, and when his big hand closed on its grip, the blood in his fist made holding the weapon nearly impossible. Even so, Longarm was able to thumb back the hammer and roll sideways three times before the second Apache charged out of the darkness with his gun bucking fire and lead.

Longarm shot the Indian at almost point-blank range. The Apache folded, but even as he was dying he was trying to get his gun up and shoot again.

"Sorry," Longarm said as his boot lashed out and sent the Apache's weapon spinning into the brush. "But this time you and your friends lose."

The fight was over. Longarm felt weak and had one hell of a tough time getting the knife wounds to stop bleeding. Maybe, though, that was good because it would prevent any poisoning. Once the wounds were bandaged, he longed to go to sleep but knew that he dared not.

Instead, Longarm returned to the caves and filled two canteens of water. He reloaded his six-gun, picked up the Winchester, and checked to make sure that Dan was still alive.

"I'll be back before sunrise with at least a couple of their horses," he told the old man. "And then we'll get you back to Wickenburg and a doctor. If you can hear me, just hang on, Preacher. No need for you to go to the Promised Land quite so soon."

Dan's eyelids raised and the old fella actually managed a smile. "I'm ready to die," he said. "Dammit, Marshal, don't keep me from the pearly gates · of heaven."

"I'll be back soon," Longarm said with a sigh of relief. "I don't think your time has come yet."

When Longarm stood up, he felt weak in the knees and somewhat dizzy. He shook himself and decided that he needed a bite to eat before setting off after those horses. He found some hard biscuits and salt pork and had himself a meal, squatting beside Dan and trying to still the buzzing in his head.

"Thanks," the prospector said. "For saving our lives."

"You did your part," Longarm told the man. "You were the giant killer. I couldn't have handled him on top of the rest."

"I don't believe it," Dan said. "There were five and we're both still alive, so that means you killed four of them all by yourself."

"I had some luck."

"No," Dan whispered, "luck had nothing to do with it."

Longarm saw no point in wasting either time or energy in discussion, so he washed his food down with water and headed off into the desert. The moon was just a thin wedge, but he figured it was bright enough to lead him to the outlaw horses that would carry them back to Wickenburg.

Chapter 14

Longarm walked all night across the desert. By daybreak, he was footsore and exhausted but determined not to give up his quest to overtake the five runaway horses. He was also pretty sure that the animals were waiting at the hidden springs where Preacher Dan had once found gold.

The sun was well up on the horizon when Longarm finally came to the place in the mountains which hid the secret desert springs. And, sure enough, there were the five outlaw horses, grazing on the lush green grass that surrounded the water hole. They were still saddled and bridled but had all broken their reins. When the animals saw Longarm, he was afraid that they might bolt and run, but they didn't. They seemed to realize that this was the only water for miles around, so Longarm had no difficulty in catching all but the two Indian ponies which he did not want anyway.

"Glad that you are showing more sense," Longarm said, tightening the cinch on a large sorrel gelding after he'd tied the two other captured horses to his saddle horn. " 'Cause, if you'd tried to run away, I might have lost my temper and shot the three of you."

The horses didn't seem too concerned with Longarm's empty threat. And so, after refilling his canteens, Longarm mounted the sorrel and led the extra pair back out into the desert. It was hot but not unbearable, and they made good time back to Preacher Dan and what he now thought of as the Spanish treasure caves.

After tying up the animals very securely, Longarm hurried up to check on Dan. He was relieved to see that the old prospector was still alive.

"I didn't expect to see you so soon," Dan whispered, his voice weak.

"We're getting you back to Wickenburg," Longarm promised. "Think you can make it?"

"No."

"Dammit, you had better try," Longarm gritted. "If you die on the way, I'll dump your body off and the coyotes will feast on it tonight."

It was a poor attempt at humor, but Dan managed a smile nonetheless. "I'll make it," he said. "What about food and water?"

"I'll pack all that I can on the two extra horses."

"I want you to poke around in these caves just a little more," Dan urged.

"For what?"

"I dunno. I just have a feeling that old Jimmy Cox must have had time to bury most of his Spanish gold coins. I've had little else to do but think since you left yesterday, and I believe that I have things figured."

"What things?"

"Where Jimmy would hide his gold coins."

"I'm listening," Longarm said.

"I think that he hid them in that second cave. You know, the one way back in this hillside."

"What makes you think so?"

"Because that's exactly where I'd hide them. And I'd bury them in the floor and then smooth it over with dust. Marshal, you need to check out that floor."

"It's too big to go over, and besides," Longarm replied, "I need to get you to a doctor."

"Ain't no *real* doctor in Wickenburg," Dan told him. "Just a tooth puller."

"Well," Longarm said, "there will be medicine and a better place for you to rest. Also, if you die, there's a still half-empty cemetery in Wickenburg and probably an undertaker who needs the cash."

Dan chuckled drily. "Damned if you don't have a soft spot in your heart after all, Marshal!"

"I had better start preparing a travois for you," Longarm said. "Unless you can sit up in the saddle."

"Not a chance," Dan replied. "But first, I'd like you to go check out the floor of the second cave."

"You seem mighty persistent on this matter. Are you holding back some information on me?"

"No. But I prayed some on this matter and I do believe in the power of prayer."

"Don't tell me that God told you that's where Jimmy buried his treasure."

"All right," Dan confessed, "Jimmy did hint around about a second, deeper cave and that it was, to use his words, 'worth taking a good look at' if anything happened to him. I just figure he said that to tell me where the Spanish treasure is buried."

Longarm's eyes widened. "Dammit, why didn't you tell me this before?!"

" 'Cause I was planning to find those hidden coins for myself and use them for charitable works. And, if *you* find them, I expect you to do the same."

"Some," Longarm agreed, "but not all."

"Most."

"Fair enough."

He left Dan and found a shovel, then Longarm crawled back into the second cave which he'd already found so interesting. Lighting a kerosene lamp, he started at one end of the cavern and worked his way to the other, moving very slowly back and forth on his hands and knees.

Longarm wasn't sure how he would know when he located a spot where Jimmy might have buried the gold coins. But less than an hour later, with his fingers brushing back and forth across the dusty floor, he felt something unusual. Longarm froze for a moment, then he brushed the dust aside and saw that there was a large metal box whose top was buried just a fraction of an inch below the floor's uneven surface.

"Eureka!" he exclaimed, brushing the dirt away and discovering an old treasure chest.

A moment later, he was prying up the lid and, sure enough, there were hundreds of Spanish gold coins gleaming up in his lamplight, pretty as an Arizona sunset.

"Holy Moses!" Longarm whispered, dipping his big hand into the treasure box and allowing the coins to slip between his fingers. "There must be five hundred of them!"

Longarm did not know what the coins were worth, but he expected it was in the tens of thousands of dollars, given their historical value. Even in terms of their pure gold weight, they were worth more money than he'd earn in many years.

"Jimmy. Jimmy," Longarm whispered, rubbing a particularly large coin balanced between his thumb and index finger. "I sure wish you were here with me now to at least see that you didn't die entirely in vain."

Longarm used his knife to dig out the old Spanish treasure chest. It was somewhat rusted but still intact. He carried it back to Dan.

"So," the preacher said, "we found it!"

"Yes, take a good look."

Dan's eyes widened with surprise and pleasure when he saw how many coins were in the treasure box. Sniffling and then rubbing away a few tears, he said, "Do you realize how much good and charitable work this will pay for? Why, there are churches, schools, old hungry people and orphans whose lives will be changed by this treasure."

"I said I was going to take . . . a little of it for myself," Longarm reminded the preacher.

"Of course! And I would not have it any other way. After all, you risked your life for me and for this bounty. It would be only right, even if you *are* a federal marshal working in the line of duty."

"What is *that* supposed to mean?" Longarm asked with a sudden scowl.

"Oh, nothing! Nothing at all. It's just that . . . well, I sort of think that you are on the government payroll. I mean, you're getting paid every day we are here, aren't you?"

"Why sure! In the neighborhood of a whole damned dollar a day."

"Well, then, as a government *servant*, I just kind of

123

thought that you might want to donate whatever little share you think you are due of this treasure to charity."

"You're wrong because I don't."

"Fine! Be that way." Dan smiled but without warmth. "So I guess now we need to get back to Wickenburg before we have any more visitors. Huh?"

"That's right."

"With me on a travois."

"Right again." Longarm came to his feet. "I'll start preparing for our trip out of this hell. There's an old axe that the outlaws were using to chop wood. It's dull but I can use a few mining timbers for the long extensions on the travois. There's blankets and canvas aplenty to rig up for you to lie down upon."

"Then we're leaving soon?"

"At sundown," Longarm told the man. "Actually, I think I'll make *two* travois for the two extra horses to drag. You'll be on one and I'll pack out our food, water, and that Spanish treasure box on the other."

"What about the bodies?"

Longarm frowned. "I'll bury them under another rock slide. If you want to crawl over to them and say a few prayers, that's up to you. I don't care one way or the other. They wouldn't have given us a burial."

"I suppose not."

"I *know* not," Longarm said.

With that, he went and got the axe, which he used to cut four long timbers. They were made of cedar and hard as nails, so Longarm knew that they would serve well as travois poles. It took him less than an hour to complete both travois and then to grain and water the horses.

After that, he loaded the extra travois with as much water as he could, then food, and covered it all with a piece of gray canvas and lashed it down tight.

"All right, horses," he said. "We're going to hitch these travois up to your saddles and you're not going to give me any trouble. Is that clearly understood?"

The two horses proved to be calm and cooperative, but even at that, Longarm took no chances. In addition to keeping them tied to the sorrel's saddle horn, he hobbled them both until both had accepted the travois.

After that, Longarm dragged the bodies of the five outlaws over to another hillside and created another rock slide to cover them up forever. It was a dirty, gruesome job. Especially considering the giant that Dan had beheaded with a powerful blast from the big shotgun. Burying the dead this way was a trick that he had often used. With tons of loose shale over the bodies, they would never be found or disturbed by wild animals.

"You got 'em buried, huh?"

"Yeah," Longarm said. "You want to give 'em the last rites?"

"I guess not," Dan replied.

"Let's have ourselves something to eat and then get out of here," Longarm decided out loud. "This place is too familiar with the dead."

"I was thinking the same thing. Marshal, how many Spaniards do you think died here?"

"I have no idea."

"You couldn't tell anything from the bones?"

"I counted six different skulls, but it wouldn't surprise me if the coyotes had carried a whole lot more than that out of the caves and then scattered them out in the desert."

"I wonder what went wrong."

"What do you mean?"

"I mean," Dan said, "that this must have been some important exploration party. Maybe a party set out by

Coronado or some other important Spanish explorer.''

"I have no idea," Longarm said. "I can't even imagine why they would have carried gold coins."

"To buy favors or peace from the hostile Indians they expected to come across, I'd guess."

"Yeah, that makes sense," Longarm said. "I wonder if the Indians had a role in their undoing."

"Probably."

Longarm looked closer at the old man. "Why do you say that?"

"Because," Dan reasoned, "if the Apache or whatever bunch that were in these parts at the time were friendly, they would have saved the Spaniards. They would have known how to survive and find water and whatever else they needed. But the fact that they *didn't* save the Spaniards tells me that they considered them to be enemies."

Longarm figured that made a lot of sense. He didn't know much about the history of exploration in the American Southwest, but he did know that the Spaniards had penetrated very deep into this country in search of the legendary Seven Lost Cities of Gold. They'd already plundered the Incan and Mayan cultures in Peru and Mexico and taken immense fortunes. No doubt, their previous successes had convinced them that they would find even more riches in the Southwest. That expectation, however, had proved to be their fatal undoing. The Apache, Mojave, Pima, and other Arizona tribes were all as poor as church mice and not known to collect gold or silver.

"Marshal?"

"Yes?"

"Let's go. Help me onto that travois and let's get back to Wickenburg."

That would suit Longarm just fine. He still had a job to do concerning Hank Bass and knew that his boss, Billy Vail, would be more than a little upset because of this latest long absence of communication. Longarm decided to telegraph Billy as soon as he reached Wickenburg, then get right after Hank Bass. With luck, he'd track the outlaw leader down in a week, two at the most, and then wrap this whole bloody business up tight.

"Here you go," Longarm said, easing Dan onto the travois and then carefully tying him down with strips of leather.

"I don't need to be tied down!"

"Sure you do," Longarm argued. "We're going over some real rough country. Country rough enough to bounce you off the travois. My eyes will be turned ahead, not behind watching out for you."

"Are you suggesting that I could bounce off and you'd never know it?"

"That's right. That could very easily happen and I'd be in such a hurry that I'd go miles before I discovered you were missing. That being the case, I doubt that I'd even bother to come back for you, Preacher."

Dan didn't fail to note the glint in Longarm's eyes and he wasn't a bit worried. "You just get in the saddle and head us for Wickenburg," he said. "I'll stay put on this thing."

"Fair enough," Longarm replied as he mounted the big sorrel and rode off, leading the two extra outlaw horses.

The sun was fading on the western horizon, and Longarm was full of admiration and even relief and gratitude. He was sorry that his old friend Jimmy Cox was dead, probably tortured mercilessly before his sad end. But Jimmy's killers, with the sole exception of Hank Bass, had all paid the ultimate price with their own lives. Furthermore, *all* of the Spanish treasure would be used for charities. Longarm realized that, maybe except for a few coins, he'd give everything to Preacher Dan.

After all, he *was* a public servant. Underpaid, overworked but damned happy with his own humble role in life, unlike a lot of much wealthier men.

Chapter 15

The trip back to Wickenburg was slow but happily uneventful. Longarm tried to pick the easiest trails, but there were many times when he was forced to cross dry arroyos and other obstacles which gave the badly injured preacher a very difficult time. But the old codger never once complained, and although he was very weak, he was obviously on the mend by the time that they arrived in Wickenburg very late one warm evening.

"Don't get the tooth puller!" Dan gritted. "Just get me to bed and maybe a little whiskey to thicken my blood."

"Sure," Longarm said with a wink, "but I never knew a drinking preacher before."

"And you probably never knew one as shot up as me," Dan grunted.

"That's for certain. Here's the Trevor House," Longarm said, drawing his sorrel up to the closest hitching rail and then wearily climbing out of his saddle. "I'll get us a couple of rooms, Dan."

But Dan had fallen fast asleep. Longarm thought that was just fine. Sleep was an essential part of healing, so Longarm made sure that his old friend was comfortable and that the Spanish treasure box was still wrapped in canvas so that it would not attract any attention, then went inside the hotel.

There was no one behind the desk, so Longarm rang the bell loudly for several minutes until a sleepy-eyed clerk appeared. The clerk's expression was sullen and uncooperative until he recognized Longarm, and even then he had a tough time mustering a smile.

"Welcome back to town, Marshal. You . . . you look like you've traveled a long hard trail."

"I have," Longarm said. "I need a room—no, two rooms. Make them adjoining."

"You have a friend?" the clerk asked.

"Yes. Preacher Dan, who has been shot."

"So have you," the clerk said, coming awake fast. "What in the name of . . ."

"The rooms," Longarm interrupted shortly. "I'm in no mood for talk tonight."

"Of course!"

Longarm got his two rooms and went outside, where he unlashed Dan from the travois and then carried him back into the hotel. Dan hardly weighed anything and it was easy enough to get him to bed. After that, Longarm hurried back outside and unlashed the Spanish treasure box. He was glad that he had wrapped it in canvas because his appearance had caused some excitement even at this late hour. A couple of men, watching with intense curiosity, even volunteered to help Longarm carry in his belongings.

"No thanks," Longarm growled. "Why don't you boys all go back to your business, whatever that might be at this late hour."

"You find the Spanish treasure?"

"No," Longarm lied.

"Who shot you and old Dan up so bad?" another asked.

"Someone who got a fatal case of the curiosities," Longarm replied testily.

The man and his friends hastily retreated. Longarm hauled all of his valuables into the rooms and then went back out once more to water the horses and give them the last of the grain he had in his saddlebags.

"I'm sorry I can't unsaddle you and put you in some pen to roll around in tonight," he told the weary animals, "but I'll make up for it tomorrow morning."

Longarm made sure that each horse was taken care of and then, feeling his own exhaustion, he trudged back into the hotel, wanting nothing more than a hot bath, a bottle of whiskey, and then a long, restful sleep.

"Marshal?"

"Yeah?" he said, turning to the clerk.

"I suppose that it's too much to hope that you will pay for your stay here with more Spanish gold coins."

Longarm paused in the middle of the lobby. In truth, he wasn't sure *how* he would pay for the rooms, but neither was he worried. It was something he could think about after a few days when his mind and body had rested.

"What about Mr. Potter?"

"The banker?"

"That's right."

"He died of his gunshot wounds."

"Did they ever reopen his bank?"

"As a matter of fact, they did," the clerk said.

This was good news. Maybe now Longarm could finally get his hands on the government travel money that Billy Vail had promised to wire.

"And what about the banker's fiancée, Miss Victoria Hathaway?"

"The one you rescued."

"The same."

"Well," the clerk said, "after you left, she rested for a few days then traveled up to Prescott for her fiancé's funeral. She looked very weak and tired, but insisted that she be there when her fiancé was put to his final rest."

"Then what did she do?"

"Miss Hathaway returned here and, as far as I know, she is recuperating with a friend over on Third Street."

"With a lady friend?"

"Of course!" The clerk looked shocked by this question, but the hour was late and Longarm was in no frame of mind to be subtle.

"Who is this lady?"

"Her name is Ann Reed and she is a widow. Considerably older, I might add, but quite popular here in Wickenburg because of her good deeds and work—"

"How can I find them?" Longarm interrupted.

"Mrs. Reed lives in a small but comfortable brown and white painted Victorian. It's on Third Street, just a block north and two blocks west."

"Thanks."

"Shame about Mr. Potter," the clerk said as Longarm was about to go. "He was a fine, well-respected man in this part of Arizona. Very successful too. I'm sure that Miss Hathaway is deep in grieving."

"I'm sure that she is," Longarm replied.

"Oh, one other thing," the clerk said. "It's none of

my business, but everyone knows that you and Preacher Dan went out hoping to discover that lost Spanish treasure. I don't mean to pry, but—"

"Then *don't*," Longarm said coldly. "Just send up a couple of bottles of whiskey and a hot bath."

The desk clerk blushed. "Sure, Marshal," he snapped as he turned to holler for someone other than himself to start heating up the bathwater.

Longarm went back to check on Dan. The old prospector and preacher was pale and needed food and rest, but a little whiskey first might be just the tonic he required. Longarm figured he was in need of some whiskey too. It had been a rough damned week but not a bad one. They'd found the Spanish gold, put the mysterious disappearance of Jimmy Cox sadly to rest, and he'd killed five outlaws. Other than Hank Bass himself getting away, everything had gone extremely well and Longarm knew that he had no complaints coming.

There was a door connecting their two rooms, and Longarm left it open. It took nearly an hour for the bath to be drawn and his tub filled, but Longarm didn't mind. He sipped whiskey and rested, then took his bath and felt like a new man. Tomorrow, he'd shave and get a badly needed haircut and fresh change of clothes after he figured out a way to get his government money sent from Prescott. Until then, he could sell the two extra horses and saddles and get by just fine.

Longarm fell asleep within seconds after he climbed into bed. He ached everywhere and couldn't remember when he'd been any more beat and scratched up than he was now. But tomorrow everything was going to start getting better.

Much, much better.

• • •

Longarm awoke just before dawn hearing movement in Dan's adjoining room. He heard whispered voices, then a boot bump into a table or chair followed by a low oath.

Longarm reached for his six-gun, which was hanging on the bedpost. He eased the gun out of its holster and then slipped off the bed, figuring that the intruders were after the Spanish treasure. Well, they were going to get a lot more than they bargained for when he stepped into Dan's room with his six-gun in his fist.

"Dammit!" one of the men hissed. "I can't see anything in here because it's so dark!"

"Hey!" another cried. "I found something. It feels like . . . like an old metal box! And it's real heavy!"

"Where?!"

"Over here!"

"Dammit, light a match but watch out! If that big marshal wakes up, we're going to have to kill him before he kills us first."

Longarm stifled a grunt of pain as he began to tiptoe forward toward the adjoining doorway. It *was* dark, and when he reached the door, he paused for several moments until a match flared and Dan's room suddenly became illuminated.

There were *three* men, and one of them was Hank Bass! Longarm couldn't help but grin as he raised his gun and said, "All right, boys, party is over. Throw up your hands!"

Bass jumped behind one of his companions and opened fire. Longarm shot the unfortunate man that Bass was using as a shield but had to duck back into his room for cover. In the next few moments, all hell broke loose. The match went out and the rooms were plunged into darkness. Longarm dropped to the floor and fired blindly into Dan's room, more than a little afraid of accidently hitting the preacher, especially if the gunfire roused old Dan and he tried to leave his bed.

Glass shattered but Longarm was still getting return fire until he took a bead on a muzzle flash and ended the fight. A low grunt of pain and then the sound of a body striking the floor confirmed that a second outlaw was either wounded or dead. But that was a very important *or*, so Longarm wasted precious moments holding his breath and trying to figure out whether or not it was safe to enter Dan's bullet-riddled room.

"Dan! Dan, are you all right?!"

When there was no answer, Longarm felt a chill of dread pass through his body. He took a deep breath and rushed into his friend's room still half expecting to be shot at by one of the fallen outlaws.

Longarm put a match to Dan's bedside lamp and sighed with relief. Dan had apparently drunk a good deal of his own bottle of whiskey and had fallen back into a very profound slumber. Fact was, he'd slept through the entire fray and was *still* asleep. Longarm made sure of that after taking Dan's pulse and finding it both slow and steady. The lid of the treasure box was open and there were gold coins spilled across the floor and over to the shattered window.

Bass could not have taken more than a handful of the Spanish coins but, dammit, the outlaw had escaped again. His human shield was riddled with Longarm's slugs, and the other man that Longarm had dropped was barely alive. Knowing that the dying outlaw might be able to give him a few important clues as to where Bass might go, Longarm tried to plug up a hole in his chest and revive him with a few gulps of whiskey.

"Who are you?!" Longarm demanded when the dying outlaw's eyes fluttered open. "Where did Bass go?"

In reply, the outlaw tried to spit in Longarm's face. Dropping the man's head back to the floor with a loud thunk, Longarm watched as the outlaw's body began to convulse and his boot heels pounded the wooden floor. There would be no answers from this man. None at all.

Longarm collected the scattered gold coins and returned them to the metal box. He grabbed up the whiskey and took a deep drink, then heard many footsteps pounding up the hallway.

"It's over!" Longarm said, pushing the treasure box under Dan's bed. "I'm a United States marshal and I want everyone to go back to bed!"

There was some disgruntled talk in the hallway, but things quickly quieted down. Longarm regarded the two dead men and, because he knew it would be hopeless to try to catch Bass, he went back to bed himself.

Chapter 16

When Longarm awoke late the next morning, there was a small crowd down in the street near his horses. Longarm yawned and peered at them through his window. When the crowd noticed him, one of its members pointed and shouted.

"There he is! It's the marshal!"

Longarm pulled the curtain shut and went next door into Dan's room. The preacher was snoring away and his color was quite good. Longarm checked Dan's whiskey and discovered that the level of the bottle had dropped several inches. In fact, the better part of it had been consumed, telling Longarm that, preacher or not, Dan had a strong appetite for liquor.

The outlaws were still lying on the floor, and Longarm determined that his first order of business should be to remove them to the hallway where an undertaker could take care of that unpleasant business.

Opening Dan's door, he dragged the two men out to the hallway where he immediately confronted the hotel clerk and an older man who identified himself as the owner of the Trevor House.

"My name is Tidwell," the man said. "And, Marshal, I'm afraid that I'm going to have to ask you and your friend to leave this establishment at once."

"Oh? And why should I do that?"

Tidwell was a large, heavy man with a red bulbous nose and gray hair. He had probably once been quite an imposing figure, but now he just looked old and bloated. Even so, he was not a man who was afraid of expressing his thoughts.

"My hotel is my livelihood, sir. You come here and, in one night, destroy the reputation that I have created for this hotel over the past twenty years! We have never had so much as a brawl, let alone two killings!"

"I'm sorry, Mr. Tidwell, but I had no choice. These dead men broke into our room in the middle of the night and would have killed both of us except—"

"Except that you killed them first."

"That's right." Longarm's own tone of voice took on a hard edge. "It was self-defense, Mr. Tidwell, and I acted in the line of duty."

"Fine! But do your line of duty somewhere else," Tidwell snapped. "Marshal, you and your wounded friend are no longer welcome in this hotel. Please find other accommodations."

Longarm had a very powerful urge to tell this over-stuffed and self-important man to go to hell. On the other hand, he knew that his presence was a magnet for trouble. Tidwell obviously wanted to attract a high cal-iber of guests, and the fact that two men had just died in this hotel was not likely to help him achieve his aims.

138

"All right," Longarm said. "We'll leave as soon as we can find another couple of rooms."

"No," Tidwell insisted, "you'll leave *now*."

Longarm almost grabbed Tidwell by the shirtfront but somehow managed to control his anger enough to repeat, "When we find another place to stay, we'll leave. But not until then, Mr. Tidwell. I hope you understand."

"I don't, and I doubt very much if you can find any hotel in Wickenburg that will take you in, given what occurred here last night."

"That would be unfortunate . . . for all of us," Longarm said, spinning on his boot heels and going back into his room, slamming the door shut behind him.

Longarm repacked his gear and made ready to go in search of a hotel where Dan and he could recuperate. He shaved and dug out the last clean shirt in his bag, then listened to his belly growl with hunger. Going next door, he roused Dan from his sleep and said, "I have to go out and find us someplace else to stay."

Preacher Dan's eyes were a little bloodshot from the whiskey, but his color really was quite good. He yawned and asked, "Where are we?"

"This is the Trevor House. Three men came in here last night through your window. Two of them are dead and the third was Hank Bass."

"He got away?"

"Yeah," Longarm admitted. "I'm afraid he did. And maybe worst of all, he found our treasure box and got a fistful of coins. So you can bet that he won't leave us alone."

Dan was wide-awake now. "He's got more blood-suckin' friends than a dog has fleas. What are we going to do?"

"I'm not sure yet," Longarm admitted. "I think that

139

the first thing I need to do is to get you out of danger.''

"Hell, I'm not afraid to die! I'm old and shot up already. It's you that needs a hiding place."

"I'm not in the habit of hiding," Longarm said stiffly. "Never have been."

"Then this should be a first," Dan argued. "Can't you wire your federal friends for some help?"

"I could," Longarm said, "but no one would get here before the shooting was over. That being the case, whatever will happen will happen. It's up to me."

"I'll help."

Longarm smiled. "What about your . . . aversion to taking another human being's life?"

Dan closed his eyes for a moment, then said, "I was being self-righteous and trying to make up for some past mistakes. I don't think that the Lord will condemn any man for trying to save his own hide."

"Neither do I," Longarm agreed. "And as for finding a room or—"

Longarm's words were interrupted by a faint knock on his door. He turned and shouted, "Go away!"

"It's me, Victoria Hathaway. Please let me come inside."

Longarm hurried over to open the door, and the woman immediately threw her arms around his neck and hugged him very tightly. "I heard about last night, Custis! I was so upset and worried for you."

"What about me?" Dan asked from his bed.

Longarm disengaged from the lovely woman. "Victoria, this is my friend, Preacher Dan. He and I have been through quite a lot in the last few weeks."

"I can see that you have," Victoria said, pretty eyes shifting back and forth between them. "Custis, you've lost ten or fifteen pounds."

"I suppose so."

"And you're both wounded."

"Just scratches," Longarm assured her. "But we've also been evicted, and I was just about to tell Dan to keep his eye on things while I went looking around for another place for us to stay while we sort things out and try to lick our wounds."

"I have just the place in mind," Victoria said. "That's part of the reason I came here."

"You do?"

"Yes. I'm staying with a friend and . . ."

"That won't work," Longarm said quickly. "If Hank Bass gathers more men and comes hunting for me, that would be one of the very first places he'd come. You and your friend could be shot by accident. I can't take that chance."

"Would you *please* allow me to finish?"

"All right."

"As I told you on the train, I have investments in this part of the country and one of them is a mining shack about ten miles northwest of town. There's water and a mine that has run out of gold, but not before I recouped my investment fivefold. It would be a perfect hideout for us."

"What do you mean, 'us'?"

"I mean that I won't just sit back and allow you to face Hank Bass alone. I would insist on being with you."

"Not a chance!" Longarm exclaimed. "Forget that idea. I'll find a hiding place in Wickenburg."

"No you won't," Victoria told him. "Everyone in town is scared to death of Hank Bass. No matter that you have killed most of his gang. They're still afraid and know that, given his reputation and the smell of

Spanish gold, outlaws will flock to his side."

Longarm frowned. "You paint a very grim picture."

"Hank Bass and his gang shot my fiancé to death. Never mind that I wasn't very much in love with him— he still didn't deserve to die."

"No, he did not."

"And then . . ." Victoria said, her voice catching with emotion and tears filling her pretty eyes, "they raped me as if I were some . . ."

"Stop it," Longarm said, pulling the woman to his chest and squeezing her tight. "What happened can't be changed, but what matters is that you know that you have nothing to be ashamed about. Nothing at all."

"I know," Victoria choked, "but it *would* help if Bass were dead."

"Maybe it would also help you to know that Dan and I managed to gun down his gang. The ones that violated you, Victoria."

"You did?"

"Yes." Longarm tipped her head back and used his thumb to wipe away her tears. "There's only Bass left to pay for what happened. And I swear that I'll kill him. There will be no arrest."

Victoria kissed Longarm's mouth. Kissed him hard and with great passion. When she pulled back, she whispered, "That's for what you are and what you said you'll do."

"Heavens to Betsy!" Dan exclaimed from his bed. "Can I get kissed like that too?"

"No," Longarm said with a smile. "You're too old and you're a preacher, remember?"

"Bible says nothing against getting kissed."

"Shut up," Longarm told the old man without any heat in his voice.

"My prospector's shack," Victoria said, "will be perfect, and you do need a sanctuary."

Longarm's smile faded. "I just can't allow you to come there with us, Victoria. I'm going to have enough to worry about taking care of my own problems. Can't you understand that?"

"Yes, I can."

"Then you agree?"

"All right. Whatever you say."

Longarm hugged her tightly. "Good! Now all we have to do is figure out how to get to your claim without being seen by anyone—no easy task."

"You'll have to sneak out through the back alley," Victoria said. "And maybe a diversion would help."

"What kind of a diversion?"

"I don't know. How about a fire?"

"Are you serious?" Longarm knew that fires could sweep through a clapboard town like Wickenburg in minutes. They were the scourge of all frontier settlements.

"My friend has an old barn that sits alone in the back of her yard. We could set it on fire. It wouldn't pose much of a threat to anything nearby, but the volunteer fire department would come running and so would everyone else."

"That would be perfect!"

"All right then," Victoria said. "I'll draw you a map to that mining shack and then set the fire."

"Set it at high noon," Longarm told her. "We're going to need a little time to get things ready to leave."

Victoria nodded, then she dragged a pencil and paper from her pockets and proceeded to draw Longarm a map that would lead him to her hidden mining shack in the mountains.

"Any chance you could get us a buckboard and canvas to cover Dan when we leave?" Longarm asked. "He's not up to riding a horse and—"

"Sure I am!"

"No, you're not," Longarm countered. "And a travois would leave tracks that even a half-blind man could follow."

"How about a carriage and two-horse team?" Victoria asked. "Would that be all right?"

"It would be just fine."

She sighed. "Then that is the first thing that my friend and I will do."

"Tell Mrs. Ann Reed that I'll never be able to thank her enough."

"Me neither," Dan said.

"How did you know my friend's name?"

"The desk clerk told me last night when we came in. I was going to pay you a quick visit once things settled down and I had taken care of our horses."

"Ann is a saint and I've told her all about you," Victoria said. "She also hates Hank Bass. He is the reason that she is a widow."

Longarm nodded with understanding. "It sounds to me like Bass has made a lot of widows in this part of Arizona."

"He's made his last," Victoria said with a firm set of her jaw. "And, Custis, if he kills you before you can kill him, I'll find a way to settle the score. I swear it!"

Longarm believed her. There was a lot of hatred and pain in Victoria, but also a lot of courage and determination. It was clear from the look on her pretty face and the tone of her voice that she was not bluffing.

Victoria kissed Longarm good-bye and then, because Dan looked so envious, she leaned over and gave him a nice kiss on the forehead and said, "You both watch out for each other."

"We will," Dan promised.

After Longarm was sure that he understood her map, Victoria hugged him again and then she hurried away. Longarm stood beside his window and watched her cross the street. She was even more beautiful than she was daring and courageous, and that was really saying something.

"You are a lucky dog," Dan said. "I never in all my life had a woman that pretty kiss me like she kissed you."

Longarm shrugged.

"If I had, I'd have married her," Dan said.

"She was engaged to be married."

"She's not anymore," Dan said. "But she won't last long out in this part of the country. You can bet that every eligible bachelor in northern Arizona will want to court her."

Longarm watched Victoria disappear around a building and then he turned back to Dan, smiled, and said, "You know something, I like you better when you are asleep."

Preacher Dan cackled, then closed his eyes and did go back to sleep.

Chapter 17

At high noon, the fire bell rang out sharply and Longarm went to his window to see everyone scattering down the main street of Wickenburg. A few blocks away, he watched a plume of black smoke billowing into the clear blue sky and knew that Victoria had kept her promise.

"It's time," he said, going over to help Dan. "Let's get out of here."

"What if someone comes in and takes that treasure chest while you're helping me down to the carriage?"

"Well," Longarm said, "if you want, you can hang on to it and I'll hang on to you and we won't have to worry about that."

"Sounds good," Dan grunted.

Longarm picked up the treasure chest filled with the Spanish gold coins. It probably weighed thirty pounds and he really wondered if Dan had the strength to hold it, but that doubt was soon erased. Dan hugged that treasure chest like a pretty woman, and they made their way out of the room and then down the back stairway to the alley.

"There it is," Longarm said, grinning. "Just as promised."

Longarm helped Dan into the carriage. "Lie down on the floor," he ordered, covering the man and the treasure chest up with a big purple blanket. "I've got to go back up to our room and get my rifle, shotgun, and a few other things that I can't afford to leave behind."

"Hurry back!"

"Don't worry," Longarm promised. "I'll be back before you know it."

Longarm returned to his room. He had already arranged everything he needed to take so that it only took a moment to gather his bags and weapons, then he hurried back to the alley, his mind racing as fast as his feet. He tried to prepare himself for anything that might go wrong while attempting to leave Wickenburg undetected.

The carriage was *gone*!

Longarm couldn't believe his eyes. The alley was empty. What in blazes was going on here?! He followed the tracks out into the street, still hearing the loud clanging of the fire bell. A volunteer fire company of six men pulling a water wagon careened around a corner and almost trampled Longarm. No one seemed to notice him; everyone was running toward the fire, most with buckets of sand or water. Longarm had seen this kind of panic before. Frontier towns were extremely vulnerable to being razed by infernos.

There were so many people rushing toward the fire that Longarm had some difficulty following the carriage tracks, which were already being trampled into oblivion.

Still, he could see that they were leading out of town heading north.

When Longarm reached the end of town, he staggered to a standstill and gazed out at the northern horizon. He couldn't see anything. Whoever had taken the carriage had driven it out of Wickenburg very fast and was no doubt already miles away and putting more and more distance between him and Longarm with every passing moment.

Longarm wheeled around and studied a pair of horses tied in front of a saddle shop. Stealing a horse was a hanging offense, but he was a United States marshal and had the authority to take extreme measures during times of great emergency. Well, this was sure as hell an emergency. Longarm chose what appeared to be the biggest and strongest of the pair, then used an extra few minutes to tie his saddlebags and shotgun down. Satisfied, he untied a muscular but jug-headed bay horse and climbed into the saddle with his Winchester clutched in his left hand and the reins in his right.

"Ya!" he shouted, booting the bay into a gallop.

The horse was no prizewinner, but it quickly proved it had excellent speed. Trouble was, the stirrups were far too short, so Longarm had a devil of a time riding after the carriage. Finally, he just let his feet dangle and pushed the bay gelding on to the north just as hard as it would run. And sure enough, in less than two miles he saw the distant outline of the carriage.

Longarm really worked over the bay, and the animal soon closed in on the carriage, whose team was already badly winded.

"Stop!" Longarm shouted.

The carriage slowly came to a stop, and when Longarm drew up beside it, he had his second big surprise of the day. There was no driver and the Spanish treasure box was open and empty. Dan lay sprawled and unconscious on the floor of the carriage.

"Damn!" Longarm swore, leaping from his saddle and tying the bay gelding to one of the wheels before he dragged Dan back up to the seat.

The old man had been savagely pistol-whipped. Longarm felt for Preacher Dan's pulse, afraid that someone might have finished him off once and for all. Dan was still alive. There was a canteen in the carriage, and Longarm used its contents to wet his handkerchief and then to slowly revive the unconscious preacher.

"Dan! Dan, wake up! Can you hear me?"

"Yeah," Dan whispered, his voice groggy.

"Who did this?!"

"I . . . I don't know. I was hiding under the blanket, remember?"

"And you saw or heard no one?"

"Nothin'," Dan said, still trying to focus. "I was waiting for you to come back, and then next thing I know, you're here and my head feels like it is busted."

"Someone tricked us," Longarm said, shaking his head back and forth. "The Spanish treasure box and all its gold coins are gone."

Dan's eyes popped open and he looked down between his feet at the floorboards. "Gone?"

"That's right," Longarm replied. "All gone."

"Well, who could have—"

"Maybe Victoria," Longarm said, finding it very hard to believe.

"No!"

"Then who the hell else?! Victoria Hathaway was the *only* one who knew of our plan of getting out of Wickenburg without being seen. She alone had the knowledge of how to steal the treasure box.''

"I can't believe she'd betray us."

"Me neither," Longarm admitted, shoulders slumping with dejection. "But women can be as cunning as a coyote, and there are plenty of bad ones. Maybe Victoria is one of them and her greed just got the better of her."

"You're wrong, Marshal. My guess is that she just made the mistake of telling a friend who told someone who told someone else."

"We'll find out what happened later. But right now, we need to go to that mining shack and gather our wits. Maybe I can sort things out and not make another big mistake."

"It wasn't your fault."

"Well," Longarm said, feeling rotten, "it was more my fault than anyone else's that I can think of."

"Do you think it was Hank Bass who pistol-whipped me and took the treasure box?"

"I can't think of anyone more likely," Longarm replied. "Can you?"

"No."

Longarm turned his stolen horse free and, sure enough, the ugly bay went trotting back to Wickenburg. He climbed into the carriage and drove on with Victoria's map in his hand.

"Wait here while I check this out to make sure that we don't get any more surprises," he told his friend when they drew within a few hundred yards of the mining shack.

Longarm stayed low and tried to keep out of sight as he circled around behind the shack and then crept down to it with the big shotgun clenched in his fists. The shack and the nearby mine were empty, and there was no indication that anyone had been in the vicinity in a long time. Satisfied that he was not walking into a trap, Longarm returned to the carriage and drove it up to the shack, then helped Dan inside and made him as comfortable as possible.

"It's pretty humble," he told the preacher.

"Ain't so bad," Dan commented. "I've slept in plenty of worse places. In fact, *most* places I've slept in have been worse than this shack."

Longarm looked around. There was a tin stove, some pots, pans, and eating utensils as well as a few cans of tinned goods. There was also mice shit and a thick coating of dust over everything. The cabin was quite small, less than two hundred feet square, but the roof was intact and it would offer them protection against the hard summer rain and sun.

"You take the bed," he told Dan as he went outside. "I'll get some blankets."

"Wouldn't mind having something to eat and some whiskey to wash it down with," Dan said. "My head feels like it's been hammered real hard."

"It has been," Longarm replied. "And if your skull wasn't so thick, you'd be dead."

Longarm got the fire going and boiled some beans and water for coffee. He opened a tin of peaches and fried some salt pork. Then he explored the area, finding nothing of interest. The mine went about thirty feet into solid rock, and someone had worked for a long hard time out in this desolate area. Longarm saw no signs of gold or silver, but he knew that there must have been some ore recovered from this claim or no one would have continued to work it so long or so hard. He found the usual rusty tin cans, a broken wheelbarrow, rotting rope and leather. It always amazed him how tenacious miners

151

could be once they were bitten by the gold bug. Whoever had first established this isolated mining claim must have worked it for years.

As evening approached and the shadows grew long, Longarm tried to put his setback in perspective. Sure, he'd lost the Spanish gold, but he'd track Bass down and recover it soon enough. He determined that he would ride one of the carriage horses back into Wickenburg after dark and start asking questions. That was his plan until Victoria arrived just at sundown.

"Why did you come out here?!" Longarm asked, his voice sharp with disapproval.

"To see if I could help you," she replied, dismounting. "And also to bring you some fresh supplies."

"We can get by on what we have for a few days."

Victoria's anger flashed. "After this greeting, you may have to."

"I'm sorry," Longarm said, realizing he was not being very appreciative. "But Dan and I had a very bad surprise in the alley this morning."

"What surprise?"

"Someone was aware of our plan and the diversion. The moment I left Dan, they pistol-whipped him and took the Spanish gold. They were also clever enough to drive the carriage north out of town, then leave it and escape."

"What?!"

"You heard me, Victoria. Dan has a nasty bump on his head and the gold coins are all gone."

"But who could have known about this other than the three of us?!"

"Your friend, Ann Reed."

"I'll forget you said that," Victoria replied, face turning dark with anger. "Ann would *never* betray my trust."

"Then she told someone else who took the information to Hank Bass," Longarm said. "Because someone sure as hell had to make a slip of the tongue."

Victoria expelled a deep breath. "I suppose that Ann could have had a slip of the tongue. She is so naive that she trusts everyone and has no secrets."

"All right," Longarm said, "let's give Ann the benefit of the doubt and assume that she did make a slip of the tongue and it got back to Hank Bass, who saw his golden opportunity to grab our Spanish treasure. What is done is done and it can't be helped. Tomorrow, I'd go after Bass, but I can't really leave Dan here by himself."

"Oh, sure you can!" the old preacher argued. "Marshal, I'll be fine. But I'd be even finer if your pretty friend would stay here with me."

"I can't," Victoria told him. "I'm going to help Custis find Hank Bass."

"Oh, no!" Longarm objected.

"Oh, yes," Victoria countered. "You *need* me."

"Why?"

"Because, unlike yourself, I know almost everyone in this part of Arizona and I have enough money in my saddlebags to buy the information you'll need to catch Bass."

"Marshal," Dan said, "those *are* pretty good reasons."

"Yes," Longarm had to agree, "they are. But, Victoria, things can go wrong. If you go with me, you could get shot, even killed."

Victoria's eyes flashed. "Hank Bass and his gang put me through hell and I'll do anything and everything I

153

can to see that he is brought to justice. You need my help and it serves no good purpose to be stubborn."

"All right," Longarm agreed. "But only on the condition that you do exactly as I say."

"I accept those terms," Victoria said. "When can we start searching for Hank Bass?"

"We'll leave tomorrow morning."

"Fine," Victoria said, nodding her pretty head. "Now, why don't we get some food cooking and enjoy a campfire before we turn in for the night."

Longarm thought that an excellent idea. Victoria soon proved herself to be a good cook, and it didn't hurt a bit that she had brought an apple pie out for dessert. Dan consumed most of that, and then, with a loud and satisfying belch, he fell asleep. Since the night was warm, Longarm moved his bedroll outside and stretched out underneath the starry desert sky.

"Good night, Victoria."

She came over to lie beside him. "Do we have to just go to sleep?"

"Isn't that what you'd like to do?"

Her reply was a passionate kiss. "Does that answer your question?"

"It does." Longarm studied her in the moonlight. "I just thought that, after what happened with Bass and his gang, that you'd . . ."

"I'd hate all men?"

"Yeah, something like that."

"I hate men who act like animals," Victoria said, unbuttoning Longarm's shirt. "And after what happened to me, I want to thank you in the best way I know how. You really saved my life, you know."

"I was acting in the line of duty, Victoria. You don't owe me a thing."

"Maybe not," she said, beginning to work on his belt, "but I *need* to make love to a good and brave man like you. It would . . . cleanse me. Make me feel good again. Does that make any sense at all, Custis?"

"Yes, I suppose it does," he replied, crushing her in his arms with his own passion rising to a fever.

Minutes later, they were making love, and Longarm found that he was not as tired or as battered as he'd thought. Victoria was passionate and more than eager to please. Longarm drove his rod into her and Victoria gasped with pleasure, then locked her lovely legs around his waist. After that, they both lost themselves in an intense pleasure that kept building and building until they were lunging and bucking and their passion was finally extinguished.

"You were even better than I thought you'd be," Victoria later whispered in his ear.

"You should see what I can do when I'm rested."

"I'm afraid that you'd quickly wear me out, Custis."

"It would be fun to try."

They lay content in each other's arms until almost midnight, and only once did they speak and that was when Victoria asked, "Do you think we can find Bass and kill him before he spends all that Spanish treasure?"

"I hope so."

"Me too. So much good could come of it despite its tragic history. I think that it should be used to *save* lives, or at least improve them."

"That was Dan's intention and I fully approve," Longarm said. "Poor Jimmy Cox would have just spent it all in the saloons, but Dan will put it to good purpose."

"If it isn't all gone before we recover it."

Longarm nodded and drifted off to sleep. He was too exhausted to ask Victoria where she thought they could best take up the notorious outlaw's trail. Oh, well, they could talk that over tomorrow morning.

Chapter 18

Hank Bass had vanished like smoke in a high wind. Longarm and Victoria had returned to Wickenburg and done everything in their power to gain some hint of where the man had gone to hiding. But no one knew or was about to tell on the outlaw's whereabouts. Part of it was fear, but Longarm wondered if Bass had simply holed up in some isolated place where it was very unlikely he would be found.

"He's smarter than I'd figured," Longarm said one hot afternoon as they left Tucson drifting south and asking questions of everyone they met. "Bass hasn't even spent any of those gold coins."

"If he did," Victoria said, "he knows that the news of it would spread like a wildfire."

"That's right," Longarm agreed. "But from what I can gather, Hank Bass is a man who likes to spend money on his pleasures, and so I can't imagine that he

157

would be able to hold on to those gold coins for very long. Especially after he gets down near the border and starts to romancing his señoritas."

"Custis, has it occurred to you that he might intend to ride deep into Mexico?"

"Yes, and the trouble is, I have no authority down there and in fact am not supposed to even cross the border."

"But if he *is* in Mexico, we can't just let him go free," Victoria protested. "With all that Spanish gold, he may *never* return to the United States. Why should he take the chance of being caught or arrested?"

"He wouldn't," Longarm replied. "But we've learned from asking questions that Hank Bass likes beautiful women, liquor, and gambling. Any one of those can quickly drain away all of a man's money. And I'll tell you something, the Mexicans who live near the border are experts in separating a gringo from his dollars or his gold."

"So are we going to ride all the way to the border?"

"I think that's our best hope," Longarm answered. "I don't really know what else we can do. The last information we've gotten is that Bass was seen riding south. My hunch is that he did cross the border but that he'll remain very near it. Most outlaws like to keep the border in sight—just in case some corrupt Mexican authorities attempt to extort them for their gold or American dollars."

"I see."

"I have a few old friends on both sides of the border near Nogales," Longarm said. "If our man is anywhere near there, I'll learn about it."

"Would you go deep into Mexico after him?"

"You bet I would," Longarm vowed. "After what he

did to you and others, I'd not hesitate a minute to cross the border even if it meant risking my badge."

Victoria reached out and took his hand. "I'm sure that we can find something to do while we wait for Hank Bass to come back from Old Mexico."

Longarm read the wanton look in her eyes and he knew that Victoria was right and that they would have no trouble whiling away the time. The trouble was, Longarm was not an especially patient man and neither was his boss, Billy Vail.

He'd sent a telegram to Billy from Tucson, requesting additional travel funds and also sketching out his progress on the case. He'd told Billy he'd managed to put an end to the Bass gang, but that Hank was still on the run. Billy had replied in a terse telegram that made it clear he was not very happy with Longarm's progress, but he had also forwarded another hundred dollars for travel expenses.

"Victoria," Longarm said, "I'm afraid we're about to receive some bad company."

The three riders had appeared from behind a hill. Longarm rested his shotgun across his saddle horn, just in case. This was a cruel, rugged country and he was not about to take any chances, especially in Victoria's company. She was a beauty and would be worth a small fortune to some wealthy Mexican rancher or official. The slave trade was nothing new in this desert southwest, and Longarm was making sure that he could protect Victoria.

"Trouble?" she asked, unable to hide her sudden anxiety.

"We'll find out. I gave you a pistol, why don't you slip it into your riding skirt . . . just in case."

"All right."

Longarm noticed that the three hard-looking riders reined their horses away from each other a few yards, which was definitely not a good sign. Two of them wore Mexican sombreros, but the one in the middle was a tall, bearded white man whose dress and saddle indicated he was a Texan.

"Victoria," Longarm said without taking his eyes off the approaching riders, "did you just see how they fanned out a little?"

"Yes."

"That's almost a sure giveaway that they mean bad trouble," Longarm told her.

"So what do we do?"

"Expect the worst. Damn, but I wish that I hadn't allowed you to come this far south with me!"

"I'll be all right," she replied, voice sounding high and strained but filled with resolve. "I've got the pistol in my hand now and I won't hesitate to use it."

"Let's just hope that it doesn't come to that," Longarm said as he drew in his horse and raised his hand in a gesture of peace and greeting.

The three riders didn't acknowledge the greeting, but they finally did draw in their horses. The white man wore a battered old Stetson and he thumbed it back on his brow, then stared at Victoria with a thick-lipped and lecherous smile that made Longarm's blood boil.

"Mister, do you have some problem with your eyes?" Longarm asked, ignoring the two Mexicans, who looked plenty dangerous in their own rights.

The white man finally tore his glance from Victoria and regarded Longarm. He was big, filthy, and missing his upper front teeth. Long wisps of dirty brown hair sprayed out from under his hat, and his shirt was unbuttoned almost to his navel so that his hairy chest glistened with sweat. Like the Mexicans, this man wore two pistols and had a rifle stuffed into his saddle boot. All three of them gave Longarm a cold stare that left little doubt of their sinister intentions.

"She's real pretty," the man with the Stetson finally said, grinning like a fool. "Prettiest woman I seen in a long, long time."

"She's mine," Longarm said flatly. "And we're on our way to Nogales."

"Why?"

"What do you mean?" Longarm asked.

"If I had me a woman as pretty as this, I wouldn't go anywhere! I'd just stay in bed with her until I was all fucked down to a nubbin."

Longarm had heard enough. There was no longer any question that these three men would try to kill him and take Victoria and their outfit. And since that was the case, it was always better to start the play and give yourself the edge, especially when the odds were stacked against you.

"Victoria, are you ready?" he asked softly.

"I am," Victoria said, her voice a thin whisper.

The big man cocked his head like a big vulture. "What are you both jabbering about?"

"This," Longarm said, whipping the shotgun up and pulling the trigger.

The big man was knocked flying from his horse, and when one of the Mexicans proved himself very fast with a gun, Longarm used his second load even as he heard Victoria's gun bark twice.

The battle was decided in just a few heartbeats, and then Longarm was dragging Victoria from her saddle and holding her tight.

"I feel like I'm going to get very sick," she gasped,

taking deep lungfuls of air. "I never killed anyone before."

"It's not something that you ever get used to," Longarm told her. "But you did what you had to do."

Longarm was about to say more, but the rider that Victoria had shot moved. Spinning Victoria around so that he shielded her body, Longarm put another slug in the bandito.

He holstered his gun and took Victoria back into his arms, saying, "Now you don't need to get sick because *I* killed him instead of you."

Victoria nodded but she still looked quite pale. "Can we just get out of here?"

"Sure," Longarm said. "As soon as I catch up their horses and pack them to the nearest cemetery."

"What will you do with their outfits?" Victoria asked.

"Sell 'em because I'm underpaid and need the extra cash."

Longarm reloaded his gun and then he went to round up the three horses. He soon had the bodies lashed down over their saddles, and a few hours later they delivered them to a small village named Arivaca. As expected, their appearance caused quite a stir in the little town. Longarm inquired about a local marshal and wasn't a bit surprised to learn there was none.

"You got a cemetery over yonder," he said, pointing. "Someone here must act as the undertaker."

"Mr. Blades who runs the cafe," the wizened old gent who ran the run-down livery and whose name was Willy said. "I seen them three dead ones plenty of times. Mister, you did this part of the country a favor by killing those murderin' sidewinders."

162

"I expected that I might have," Longarm replied. "You interested in buying their outfits?"

"Ain't got much money."

"It won't take much money," Longarm answered. "Willy, just pay me fifty dollars each and they're yours."

"Thirty."

"Forty or we take them on down to Nogales and double that price. The saddles are worth twenty all by themselves. And when you add in the blankets, bridles, and . . ."

"One hundred dollars and that's all the money I have in this world. I swear it is!" Willy exclaimed.

"Okay, providing you give me some information."

The old man squinted. "Information can get pretty expensive. What kind are you looking for?"

"I'm hunting for an outlaw named Hank Bass. I have reason to believe that he passed through here not long ago, probably on his way to Nogales."

"Who *are* you, stranger?"

"I'm someone who has a score to settle," Longarm answered. "And so does my lady friend."

Willy glanced over at Victoria, who solemnly nodded in agreement.

"Hank Bass did you wrong, miss?"

"Yes."

Willy shook his head. "I believe that. Hank Bass is a mean son of a bitch, if you'll pardon my bad language. He's beat up a few women in this town, but they weren't ladies like you, miss."

Victoria looked away quickly, but not before Longarm saw tears glisten in her eyes.

"Willy, how long ago was it that Hank Bass traveled through here going toward Old Mexico?"

"He only left about four, no, three days ago," Willy said after a moment of reflection. "He caused quite a commotion 'cause he was spending some real Spanish gold coins."

"Is that right?"

"For a fact. I expect the whores and the saloons all got their share for letting him raise hell."

"Did he say he was on his way into Mexico?"

"Sure did! But he'll probably never get across the border."

Longarm was caught by surprise. "Why not?"

"Because every bandito in Mexico will be watching and waiting to get him in their gun sights. You can be sure that the word is out Hank Bass is carrying a fortune in gold coins. I expect someone will ambush the fool the very minute he crosses the border."

Longarm frowned. "Bass is anything but a fool. Maybe he'll stay on this side."

"Either way, someone will come gunning for him," Willy reasoned. "Hank always came through this town with a bunch of men to back him up in any trouble. But this time, he was alone. He's a mean, tough son of a bitch, but he can't survive down here by himself. I'm telling you, stranger, someone will bushwhack him, that's for certain."

Longarm figured that Willy was right, which meant that Hank Bass needed to be overtaken as quickly as possible.

"We should push on now, Victoria."

She sighed. "I'm very tired. Couldn't we just spend one night resting?"

"You can sleep on fresh straw here in my livery for only a dollar," the old man offered. "Safer here than in one of the hotels. A whole lot quieter too."

"The horses do need a rest," Victoria argued.

"All right," Longarm reluctantly agreed. "But we'll leave very early. No need for anyone in Arivaca to even know that we were here."

"Now you're talking," the old man said as his chin bobbed up and down in agreement.

"Willy, go find me that hundred dollars. That way, I won't have to awaken you early tomorrow morning."

"That could be fatal," Willy drawled. "So I'll go get the cash right now."

The next morning, Longarm arose at first light and got his horses saddled and ready to ride. Victoria was sleeping like a baby and he felt sorry to awaken her but there was little choice. Down in this country, the outlaw trail could run cold in a hurry, and Longarm still wasn't entirely convinced that Bass wouldn't cross the border into Mexico.

It was a hard twenty-five-mile ride down to the border town of Nogales, and both Longarm as well as Victoria were badly worn down by the dust and oppressive heat by the time they had boarded their horses and found a suitable hotel room. After a meal of beans, tortillas, and warm beer, they went to bed and slept until after dark. Then Longarm got up and prepared to go out hunting for Bass.

"You're going to have to stay here," he said. "These streets are no place for a decent woman."

"But . . ."

"If I took you around to the places I'm going to visit," Longarm interrupted, "I'd be fighting off crowds of men. No, Victoria, I insist."

"But what if you run into Bass and are shot?"

"If I don't come back tonight, come looking for me

165

in the morning. Pay a couple of tough-looking men well to protect you and make your first stop at the undertaker's. But don't worry, I'll find Hank Bass and he's the one that will be getting his ticket punched for Boot Hill.''

''You sound so confident.''

''I guess I do,'' Longarm admitted. ''The fact of the matter is that I don't allow myself to think about getting shot and killed. If I did . . . well, I just don't.''

Victoria kissed him good-bye, and when Longarm got to the door, he said, ''Keep this door locked. Under no circumstances allow anyone in but me. Is that understood?''

''Yes, of course.''

''And keep your gun handy.''

''I will,'' she promised. ''Please come back to me, Custis.''

''Count on it,'' he vowed. ''But if something should happen to me and . . .''

''It won't!''

''But if it did. You go back to the livery and get the liveryman to saddle our horses. Then ride like hell back to where you came from and never look back.''

''I'm not sure that I could leave you behind.''

''Just do it!'' Longarm ordered. ''You promised you'd obey my orders if I let you come along. I expect you to keep your promise just as I've kept mine.''

''All right.''

Longarm left their hotel room and did not walk away from the door until he heard the distinct snap of the dead bolt in its lock. Satisfied, he headed out on the town. Nogales was just as wild and lawless on one side of the border as it was on the other. Longarm knew that he would be well advised to keep his hat pulled down low and his six-gun resting light in his holster. Above all, he needed to keep his United States marshal's badge under cover.

Chapter 19

Longarm was in a deadly frame of mind as he prowled the American side of the border. He kept thinking about Jimmy Cox and how badly he'd been tortured before being killed. And about Victoria and how Hank Bass had fed her to his men like so much meat to dogs. One thing for sure, he would have no qualms about killing Bass on sight.

Saloons and cantinas lined the shabby streets of Nogales. Whores, drunks, gamblers, pimps, and all manner of degenerates prowled the dirty streets. Longarm kept his chin down when men saw him coming; they parted so that he could pass.

His routine was always the same. He would enter a saloon, order a whiskey, and take a sip. Then he'd lay a dollar down and tell the bartender, "I'm looking for Hank Bass. There's twenty more of these if you can help me find him."

No one could, until Longarm asked that same question at the Blanco Bar, one of the area's most notorious watering holes known to be frequented by cutthroats, thieves, and murderers.

"What do you want to see that bastard for?" the bartender asked under his breath.

"I have a score to settle with him," Longarm said, pretty sure this man's hatred for Bass was genuine.

"So do I," the bartender replied, "but I don't have any urge to die. Do you?"

"I can handle my own business," Longarm said. "Just point him out to me."

"He's with one of our whores," the bartender said. "He went out the back door about ten minutes ago with a girl named Rita. He should be back soon enough."

"How is he dressed?"

"Gray Stetson hat, black shirt, and boots. Haven't you ever seen him before?"

"Yes, but the light is poor in here."

"You'll be able to smell the pig," the bartender said with contempt. "He'll also have a bottle of whiskey in his hand and Rita's ass in the other."

Longarm turned toward the back of the room. "That door?" he asked, pointing.

"Yes. Now move away from here so that if he plugs you first Bass don't get the notion that I said anything. And try not to shoot the gawdamn place up, all right?"

"I generally hit what I aim for," Longarm told the man.

"I sure as hell hope so. That bastard beat the hell out of me and cut off my ring finger. See that?"

Longarm studied the stub. "Why?"

"He liked the ring I was wearing! I wouldn't give it

to him so he sucker punched me and cut my damn finger off to get it!''

"Why didn't you shoot him later?"

"He's always had a lot of friends here before. But now he's alone. Just step in behind Bass and drill him in the back. Do whatever it takes but don't make a mistake."

"I won't," Longarm promised as he moved off toward the back of the room.

Almost ten agonizingly slow minutes passed until Hank Bass charged back inside the saloon, dragging a Mexican girl in his wake. She was sobbing and her lower lip was running with blood. Longarm stepped in between the whore and the outlaw, drawing his gun.

"You're under arrest, Bass. Don't move or I'll put a slug in you quicker than you can bat your eye."

Bass was even bigger than Longarm, but hard living and heavy drinking had ruined his appearance. Even so, there was an animal-like quality about him that Longarm had seen in only the worst types of men.

"You're a lawman?"

"Head for the front door under your own power, or be carried out by an undertaker," Longarm said in a low, cold voice. "Your choice, Hank."

"Hey!" Hank shouted. "This son of a bitch that is trying to arrest me is a United States marshal! Anyone in here *like* lawmen?"

Longarm realized his mistake at once. He should have pistol-whipped or even shot Hank Bass the moment he came through the back door. Now he was about to pay for his mistake.

"We're going out back," Longarm hissed, grabbing Bass by the shirt and dragging him toward the rear door. "Come on!"

But the outlaw wasn't about to be pulled out into the rear alley. He struggled and would have broken free if Longarm hadn't pistol-whipped him across the forehead so hard that his eyes crossed and his legs buckled.

"Stay back!" Longarm shouted as the mean-spirited crowd edged forward. "I mean it!"

Longarm wrapped his left arm tight around Hank Bass's neck and held off the crowd with his six-gun as he struggled out the back door. But no sooner was he outside than the crowd charged the door, and Longarm had no choice but to haul Bass up on his toes and open fire.

He didn't know how many men fell under his gun, but it must have been several. Longarm *did* know that Bass took a fusillade of bullets to his chest and belly and was leaking like a sieve by the time he could drag him around the building and empty his pockets of whatever Spanish gold coins remained. There weren't many, maybe twenty or so, but Longarm collected them as best he could in the darkness, then he sprinted off hearing shouts and more gunfire.

He wasted no more time and took no more chances. With a half dozen good lawmen, he might have stood a chance of cleaning out this festering hole of humanity. But by himself Longarm knew that he stood no chance at all. So he circled around to the front of the hotel, sprinted to their room, and pounded on the door.

"Victoria, it's me! We've got to get out of here!"

She had the door open and was instantly in his arms. Longarm rushed into the room, grabbed his rifle and shotgun, then his saddlebags, and they took off running from the hotel.

Nogales was such a lawless town that a few gunshots did not arouse much attention. And maybe some of the

Spanish gold coins were lying spilled around Hank Bass's riddled body. Whatever the reason, Longarm and Victoria had no trouble getting to the livery and then riding hard out of town.

At daybreak, they stopped on a high, windswept ridge and gazed across twenty or thirty miles of desert toward Nogales and then on to Mexico.

Only then did Victoria ask, "What about the golden coins?"

"I was able to fill my pockets, but that's all." Longarm dug out one pocketful but kept the other. "Do what you want with them."

"And what will *you* do with the ones you keep?" Victoria asked.

Longarm's mind drifted back to Denver, and to Dolly. He recalled making a promise to that woman and said, "I think I'll spend 'em all in New Orleans."

"I could go with you," Victoria offered hopefully.

"Maybe next year, if you're not married by then," he said with a half smile as he reined north and put his horse into an easy gallop. "There's always next year."

SPECIAL PREVIEW

They were the most brutal gang of cutthroats ever assembled. And during the Civil War, they sought justice outside of the law. Paying back every Yankee raid with one of their own. They rode hard, shot straight, and had their way with every willing woman west of the Mississippi. No man could stop them. No woman could resist them. And no Yankee stood a chance of living when Quantrill's Raiders rode into town . . .

BUSHWHACKERS
by B. J. Lanagan

Available in paperback from Jove Books

And now here's a special excerpt from
this thrilling new series . . .

Jackson County, Missouri, 1862

As Seth Coulter lay his pocket watch on the bedside table and blew out the lantern, he thought he saw a light outside. Walking over to the window, he pulled the curtain aside to stare out into the darkness.

On the bed alongside him the mattress creaked, and his wife, Irma, raised herself on her elbows.

"What is it, Seth?" Irma asked. "What are you lookin' at?"

"Nothin', I reckon."

"Well, you're lookin' at somethin'."

"Thought I seen a light out there, is all."

Seth continued to look through the window for a moment longer. He saw only the moon-silvered West Missouri hills.

"A light? What on earth could that be at this time of night?" Irma asked.

"Ah, don't worry about it," Seth replied, still looking through the window. "It's prob'ly just lightning bugs."

175

"Lightning bugs? Never heard of lightning bugs this early in the year."

"Well it's been a warm spring," Seth explained. Finally, he came away from the window, projecting to his wife an easiness he didn't feel. "I'm sure it's nothing," he said.

"I reckon you're right," the woman agreed. "Wisht the boys was here, though."

Seth climbed into bed. He thought of the shotgun over the fireplace mantle in the living room, and he wondered if he should go get it. He considered it for a moment, then decided against it. It would only cause Irma to ask questions, and just because he was feeling uneasy, was no reason to cause her any worry. He turned to her and smiled.

"What do you want the boys here for?" he asked. "If the boys was here, we couldn't be doin' this." Gently, he began pulling at her nightgown.

"Seth, you old fool, what do you think you're doin'?" Irma scolded. But there was a lilt of laughter in her voice, and it was husky, evidence that far from being put off by him, she welcomed his advances.

Now, any uneasiness Seth may have felt fell away as he tugged at her nightgown. Finally she sighed.

"You better let me do it," she said. "Clumsy as you are, you'll like-as-not tear it."

Irma pulled the nightgown over her head, then dropped it onto the floor beside her bed. She was forty-six years old, but a lifetime of hard work had kept her body trim, and she was proud of the fact that she was as firm now as she had been when she was twenty. She lay back on the bed and smiled up at her husband, her skin glowing silver in the splash of moonlight. Seth ran his hand down her nakedness, and she trembled under his touch. He marveled that, after so many years of marriage, she could still be so easily aroused.

Three hundred yards away from the house, Emil Slaughter, leader of a band of Jayhawkers, twisted around in his saddle to look back at the dozen or so riders with him. Their faces were fired orange in the flickering lights of the torches. Felt hats were pulled low, and they were all wearing long dusters, hanging open to provide access to the pistols which protruded from their belts. His band of followers looked, Slaughter thought, as if a fissure in the earth had suddenly opened to allow a legion of demons to escape from hell. There was about them a hint of sulphur.

A hint of sulphur. Slaughter smiled at the thought. He liked that idea. Such an illusion would strike fear into the hearts of his victims, and the more frightened they were, the easier it would be for him to do his job.

Quickly, Slaughter began assigning tasks to his men.

"You two hit the smokehouse, take ever' bit of meat they got a'curin'."

"Hope they got a couple slabs of bacon," someone said.

"I'd like a ham or two," another put in.

"You three, go into the house. Clean out the pantry, flour, corn-meal, sugar, anything they got in there. And if you see anything valuable in the house, take it too."

"What about the people inside?"

"Kill 'em," Slaughter said succinctly.

"Women, too?"

"Kill 'em all."

"What about their livestock?"

"If they got 'ny ridin' horses, we'll take 'em. The

177

plowin' animals, we'll let burn when we torch the barn.
All right, let's go."

In the bedroom Seth and Irma were oblivious to what
was going on outside. Seth was over her, driving himself
into her moist triangle. Irma's breathing was coming faster and more shallow as Seth gripped her buttocks with
his hands, pulling her up to meet him. He could feel her
fingers digging into his shoulders, and see her jiggling,
sweat-pearled breasts as her head flopped from side to
side with the pleasure she was feeling.

Suddenly Seth was aware of a wavering, golden glow
on the walls of the bedroom. A bright light was coming
through the window.

"What the hell?" he asked, interrupting the rhythm
and holding himself up from her on stiffened arms, one
hand on each side of her head.

"No, no," Irma said through clenched teeth. "Don't
stop now, don't . . ."

"Irma, my God! The barn's on fire!" Seth shouted,
as he disengaged himself.

"What?" Irma asked, now also aware of the orange
glow in the room.

Seth got out of bed and started quickly, to pull on his
trousers. Suddenly there was a crashing sound from the
front of the house as the door was smashed open.

"Seth!" Irma screamed.

Drawing up his trousers, Seth started toward the living
room and the shotgun he had over the fireplace.

"You lookin' for this, you Missouri bastard?" someone asked. He was holding Seth's shotgun.

"Who the hell are . . ." That was as far as Seth got.
His question was cut off by the roar of the shotgun as
a charge of double-aught buckshot slammed him back

against the wall. He slid down to the floor, staining the wall behind him with blood and guts from the gaping exit wounds in his back.

"Seth! My God, no!" Irma shouted, running into the living room when she heard the shotgun blast. So concerned was she about her husband that she didn't bother to put on her nightgown.

"Well, now, lookie what we got here," a beady-eyed Jayhawker said, staring at Irma's nakedness. "Boys, I'm goin' to have me some fun."

"No," Irma said, shaking now, not only in fear for her own life, but in shock from seeing her husband's lifeless body leaning against the wall.

Beady Eyes reached for Irma.

"Please," Irma whimpered. She twisted away from him. "Please."

"Listen to her beggin' me for it, boys. Lookit them titties! Damn, she's not a bad-lookin' woman, you know that?" His dark beady eyes glistened, rat-like, as he opened his pants then reached down to grab himself. His erection projected forward like a club.

"No, please, don't do this," Irma pleaded.

"You wait 'til I stick this cock in you, honey," Beady Eyes said. "Hell, you goin' to like it so much you'll think you ain't never been screwed before."

Irma turned and ran into the bedroom. The others followed her, laughing, until she was forced against the bed.

"Lookit this, boys! She's brought me right to her bed! You think this bitch ain't a'wantin' it?"

"I beg of you, if you've any kindness in you . . . Irma started, but her plea was interrupted when Beady Eyes backhanded her so savagely that she fell across the bed, her mouth filled with blood.

179

"Shut up!" he said, harshly. "I don't like my women talkin' while I'm diddlin' 'em!"

Beady Eyes came down onto the bed on top of her, then he spread her legs and forced himself roughly into her. Irma felt as if she were taking a hot poker inside her, and she cried out in pain.

"Listen to her squealin'. He's really givin' it to her," one of the observers said.

Beady Eyes wheezed and gasped as he thrust into her roughly.

"Don't wear it out none," one of the others giggled. "We'uns want our turn!"

At the beginning of his orgasm, Beady Eyes enhanced his pleasure by one extra move that was unobserved by the others. Immediately thereafter he felt the convulsive tremors of the woman beneath him, and that was all it took to trigger his final release. He surrendered himself to the sensation of fluid and energy rushing out of his body, while he groaned and twitched in orgiastic gratification.

"Look at that! He's comin' in the bitch right now!" one of the others said excitedly. "Damn! You wait 'til I get in there! I'm goin' to come in quarts!"

Beady Eyes lay still on top of her until he had spent his final twitch, then he got up. She was bleeding from a stab wound just below her left breast.

"My turn," one of the others said, already taking out his cock. He had just started toward her when he saw the wound in the woman's chest, and the flat look of her dead eyes. "What the hell?" he asked. "What happened to her?"

The second man looked over at Beady Eyes in confusion. Then he saw Beady Eyes wiping blood off the blade of his knife.

"You son of bitch!" he screamed in anger. "You kilt her!"

"Slaughter told us to kill her," Beady Eyes replied easily.

"Well, you could'a waited 'til someone else got a chance to do her before you did it, you bastard!" The second man, putting himself back into his pants, started toward Beady Eyes when, suddenly, there was the thunder of a loud pistol shot.

"What the hell is going on in here?" Slaughter yelled. He was standing just inside the bedroom door, holding a smoking pistol in his hand, glaring angrily at them.

"This son of a bitch kilt the woman while he was doin' her!"

"We didn't come here to screw," Slaughter growled. "We come here to get supplies."

"But he kilt her *while* he was screwin' her! Who would do somethin' like that?"

"Before, during, after, what difference does it make?" Slaughter asked. "As long as she's dead. Now, you've got work to do, so get out there in the pantry, like I told you, and start gatherin' up what you can. You," he said to Beady Eyes, "go through the house, take anything you think we can sell. I want to be out of here in no more'n five minutes."

"Emil, what woulda been the harm in us havin' our turn?"

Slaughter cocked the pistol and pointed it at the one who was still complaining. "The harm is, I told you not to," he said. "Now, do you want to debate the issue?"

"No, no!" the man said quickly, holding his hands out toward Slaughter. "Didn't mean nothin' by it. I was just talkin', that's all."

"Good," Slaughter said. He looked over at Beady

Eyes. "And you. If you ever pull your cock out again without me sayin' it's all right, I'll cut the goddamned thing off."

"It wasn't like you think, Emil," Beady Eyes said. "I was just tryin' to be easy on the woman, is all. I figured it would be better if she didn't know it was about to happen."

Slaughter shook his head. "You're one strange son of a bitch, you know that?" He stared at the three men for a minute, then he shook his head in disgust as he put his pistol back into his belt. "Get to work."

Beady Eyes was the last one out and as he started to leave he saw, lying on the chifforobe, a gold pocket watch. He glanced around to make sure no one was looking. Quickly, and unobserved, he slipped the gold watch into his own pocket.

This was a direct violation of Slaughter's standing orders. Anything of value found on any of their raids was to be divided equally among the whole. That meant that, by rights, he should give the watch to Slaughter, who would then sell it and divide whatever money it brought. But because it was loot, they would be limited as to where they could sell the watch. That meant it would bring much less than it was worth and by the time it was split up into twelve parts, each individual part would be minuscule. Better, by far, that he keep the watch for himself.

Feeling the weight of the watch riding comfortably in his pocket, he went into the pantry to start clearing it out.

"Lookie here!" the other man detailed for the pantry said. "This here family ate pretty damn good, I'll tell you. We've made us quite a haul: flour, coffee, sugar, onions, potatoes, beans, peas, dried peppers."

"Yeah, if they's as lucky in the smokehouse, we're goin' to feast tonight!"

The one gathering the loot came into the pantry then, holding a bulging sack. "I found some nice gold candlesticks here, too," he said. "We ought to get somethin' for them."

"You men inside! Let's go!" Slaughter's shout came to them.

The Jayhawkers in the house ran outside where Slaughter had brought everyone together. Here, they were illuminated by the flames of the already-burning barn. Two among the bunch were holding flaming torches, and they looked at Slaughter expectantly.

With a nod of his head, Slaughter said, "All right, burn the rest of the buildings now."

Watch for

**LONGARM AND THE
MAIDEN MEDUSA**

224th novel in the exciting LONGARM series
from Jove

Coming in August!